AF265395

A Month
of Sundays

A Month of *Sundays*

Stories of Love and Loss

Megan Gordon

ALLORA PRESS ° BOCA RATON

ALLORA PRESS

Boca Raton

Printed in the United States of America

First Printing, 2015

Cover Photo © 2010 Megan Gordon

ISBN 978-0-9862802-0-7

For Mitch,
For giving me wings
and the space to fly

Table of Contents

"Life has no other discipline to impose, if we would but realize it, than to accept life unquestioningly. Everything… we deny, denigrate or despise, serves to defeat us in the end. What seems nasty, painful, evil, can become a source of beauty, joy and strength, if faced with an open mind. Every moment is a golden one for him who has the vision to realize it as such."

- Henry Miller, The Henry Miller Reader

Love, In Three Acts

Act I

They met in one of those ways that only happen in college. In the middle of music and chaos and raucous laughter. She was soaked in beer. He was a little drunk. She was beautiful, outgoing and bigger than life. He was smart and grounded. And he made her laugh. Their paths crossed, they connected. For the rest of the night, everything and everyone else faded into the background; it was just the two of them.

One night, three months later, they were sitting on the small porch of his apartment, wound around each other on the single chaise lounge, looking up at an inky sky. A star flitted across the expanse, leaving a brief but bright trail behind it.

"I always think of a shooting star as a sign from someone you lost. A little wink in your direction to let you know that everything's okay," Becca said.

"I like that," Thomas said, kissing the side of her neck. "Who's winking at you?"

"My grandmother. She was an amazing woman and my best friend. I like to think she's watching over me. It makes me feel safe. Which is weird, I guess, but it does."

"Not weird at all. It's nice."

"Who's winking at you?"

He looked at the sky and took a deep breath. He tightened his arms around her and rested his chin on her shoulder. "When I was 16 my best friend, Joe, and I were hanging out in the woods behind his house. We were messing around with some firecrackers. It had been a really dry month, I guess, because all of sudden there was a fire. We both ran, and then I heard Joe scream behind me." Thomas choked up. Becca took his hand and squeezed it.

"He'd gotten his foot caught in a trap that his father had set to keep coyotes away from their yard. I tried to get it off of his leg, but I couldn't. I ran to get help. His dad got him out of the trap and took him to the hospital. He caught a staph infection and died a week later." The last words came out as a sob. Becca turned, put her arms around him and held him tight until he stopped.

And just like that, she was in love.

Two years went by. They laughed together. Cried together. They met each other's parents.

"My mom loves you," Thomas said, after he'd introduced her.

"I'm sorry my dad got drunk. Again," Becca said, after a particularly harrowing Thanksgiving dinner at her house.

And then it was senior year. The world was waiting. Becca was going to law school. She envisioned herself helping the helpless and championing the underdog. When she thought about her future, a wave of happiness washed over her. And always, Thomas was a part of it.

"Becca, will you please just pick a movie already," Thomas snapped at her one Saturday afternoon in the spring of their last year.

She ignored his tone. "I'm having trouble deciding between these two," she said. "Which one do you want to see?"

"I don't care."

This was new. But semester exams were coming up and the pressure was on both of them, so she brushed it off. She was caught up in school and her never-ending family drama, too preoccupied to pursue it.

ooo

"I love you, but I'm not in love with you."

Becca flinched as Thomas' words slammed into her chest. He spoke them with tenderness and care, but it didn't matter. They hurt. Her chest tightened. It was hard to breathe. Two years gone with ten little words.

An hour ago they'd been at a party. Dancing. Happy. Everything seemed as it always had. She'd expected to go to his place, where they usually spent the weekends. But here, on her own bed, her heart was cracking open. She looked him in the eye, willing herself not to cry. She said nothing. There was nothing to say. No argument to be made. He wasn't in love with her. It was done.

"I'm sorry," he said, reaching for her.

"Me too," she said, avoiding his touch.

"Becca…"

She put her hand up. "Stop. There's nothing you can say to make this better."

"But…"

"Please go."

He nodded and left.

She hadn't seen it coming. The declaration that all she thought to be true wasn't. She was knocked off balance, feeling out of control. Losing control scared her to death.

And she loved him. With all of her heart. She couldn't imagine her life without him; he was the other half of her soul.

She was gutted.

Act II

She was the only one he wanted to see at this reunion. Had it really been 20 years? Twenty years since he'd seen her face or touched her shoulder. God, he missed her. *Your choice, buddy*, he thought. *It didn't have to be this way.* And yet he did the best he knew how at the time.

It only took a half an hour for Thomas to spot Becca. He'd made sure she was coming. He didn't care about the reunion. He just wanted an excuse to see her again, to talk to her.

She was standing near the bar talking to a few women that he thought he recognized. He held his breath and tapped her shoulder lightly.

She turned to him. He smiled. "Hi," he said.

Her face registered surprise, then something like panic. "Thomas… Hi." She did not move to hug him.

He thought better of trying to hug her, although he desperately wanted to. "I can't believe you're here," he said.

She shrugged. "I am." A pause. "You look good; how have you been?" She seemed uncomfortable.

"Okay, I guess. I managed to find a career that hasn't crushed my soul. You? You look amazing, by the way. You haven't changed a bit."

She blushed. "Thank you. I've been really good. I'm working for a non-profit, providing legal assistance to low-income people. I love it. I'm married to the man of my dreams—we have two sons, 10 and 13." She stopped and looked around the room for a moment before looking back at him. "Um, how about you? Are you married?"

He nodded. "For the moment. Tandy and I are separated. The divorce should be finalized soon." He half-laughed. "I guess that's what happens when you marry someone three weeks after you meet. Thankfully, there are no kids."

"I'm sorry to hear that, Thomas. Really."

"Thanks."

"It was good to see you. Good luck," she said, touching him on the forearm before she walked away.

ooo

"You are out of my league," he told her on their second date.

"It's my league; I get to choose who's in it," she replied with a mock scowl. "So shut up."

And just like that, he was in love.

He was happy with Becca, and loved the life they had together in school. The future was simply an abstract.

Thomas majored in liberal arts because he had no idea what he wanted to do. Four years slipped by quickly, but he still didn't have a direction. He was adrift. And scared out of his mind. Something would come up, he thought. In the meantime he chose not to think about it.

But it hung in the background, haunting him. As graduation loomed closer, he became more agitated and restless. He was irritable and short-tempered with Becca for no reason.

He found himself looking at other girls and wondering what it would be like to be with them. That hadn't happened since the night he'd met Becca. He'd always thought she was his future, but now everything beyond graduation was murky and dim. When she talked about living together he listened and gave vague responses. The thought scared the hell out of him. Is first love supposed to be forever?

As he walked away from her that night, he longed to turn back, to apologize, to say it had all been a lie. The farther he got, the more it tugged at him. He couldn't imagine his life without Becca. But he needed to figure out what that life would be. In his heart he felt that they'd still be friends, and, one day, they would find their way back to each other. He needed to give her some time. So he waited.

She never called.

ooo

Now he watched her walk away again, this time possibly for good. And although he'd been living it for 20 years, he couldn't imagine a life without her. Time was running out; if she left the ballroom without him, he'd never see her again.

He kept his distance, watching her. When she emerged from the ladies' room alone, he was waiting for her.

"What are you doing?" she said. Angry.

"I need to talk to you," he said. His eyes pleaded with her. "Please."

She looked across the room at her friends. They were talking and laughing and dancing. She could spare a few minutes without being missed.

She nodded. "One minute."

They walked outside into the warm night air. The lights from the hotel obscured the stars, but they both looked up anyway.

Thomas took a deep breath, and, still looking at the sky, said, "It was a lie."

She turned to him. "What?"

"When I told you I wasn't in love with you it was a lie. I didn't know it at the time, but it was. It took me years to realize that everything I was feeling had nothing to do with you. I was terrified about my life, Becca. Paralyzed. I guess I needed a distraction; I started looking at other girls. Then I felt guilty and thought that I couldn't possibly be in love with you if I was doing that. But the thought of hurting you was more than I could take. So I did nothing. Until I couldn't lie to you anymore."

She nodded slowly. "That's why you were distant and crabby sometimes. It was like you were two different people: the Thomas I loved, and some asshole who took over Thomas' body."

They both looked up at the sky again. "I'm sorry," he said.

She turned back to him. "You know, you actually did me a favor. I just threw myself into law school, made law review and graduated *summa*, which got me an internship at a firm people would have killed to get in, and got offered a job there when I passed the bar. I didn't date the whole time—I just worked. During my internship I met my husband. We've been together ever since." She paused, looking up again.

"I'm happy. For a while I thought I never would be again, but here I am. I've always wondered if we'd stayed together, would I have lost myself in you? I knew you were struggling. I was going to help you. I was ready to give up my dreams to help you find yours. That wouldn't have ended well. I'm sure of it. So don't be sorry."

"Can I be sorry that I hurt you?"

She thought for a moment. "Okay. Apology accepted."

They stood in silence.

"I still love you," Thomas said. "I always will."

Still looking at the sky she said, "I love you too. But not the same as I did. And not you, really. I love the Thomas that I knew 20 years ago. He doesn't exist anymore."

"He's in here somewhere."

"Yeah. And it's 22-year-old Becca that loves him. But she's not me."

"Becca…"

She held up her hand. "I don't know what you're looking for, Thomas. I've forgiven you. I did that a long time ago. That's all I have for you."

Act III

"Thomas McAfee was my first love. The kind of first love you dream about once you start noticing boys. I'd like to say that I knew from the first time I saw him, but I don't exactly remember when that was. That moment isn't what sticks in my mind when I think of Thomas. The first thing I remember about him is that he made me laugh. We laughed a lot, about life, death and everything in between.

"He was not like any other guy I'd met—there was always a wisdom about him, a centeredness. Like he knew something that no one else did, but he couldn't tell you about it because you weren't ready, so he just shared the essence of it. No matter what I was going through, no matter what was happening around me, Thomas was the calm in the midst of the storm, a lifeline."

ooo

Becca hovered the cursor over the "add friend" button. It had been a month since she'd seen him at the reunion; the way she left things had been bothering her ever since. It bothered her because she'd been abrupt with him, and it bothered her because something was telling her that their relationship had not reached its end yet. She clicked the button. Would he accept? And if so, what would that mean?

Jack, Becca's husband, had suggested she look for Thomas on Facebook. He thought that it would make her feel better if she could check in with her ex once in a while and know that he was okay. Becca had laughed at the suggestion; Jack knew her too well.

Two days later, Thomas had accepted her request, adding a brief note: How ridiculous and how strange to be surprised at anything which happens in life. She wrote back: Quoting Marcus Aurelius? I would have guessed Oscar Wilde. He replied: I've mellowed in my old age. So - why? *Because if you died and I didn't know what happened to you I'd never forgive myself,* she thought. She wrote: It's Facebook. That's what you do.

For months their new relationship consisted of a like here and there, a comment about her kids or his dog. Distant, but cordial.

New Message from Becca
Becca: My husband is dead.
Thomas: Becca… I'm so sorry. Do you want to talk about it?
Becca: Not really.
Thomas: What do you want to talk about?
Becca: It was an accident. Drunk driver.
Thomas: Damn. Are you alone?
Becca: I am now.
Thomas: Is there someone there with you? Your mom? Your sister?
Becca: Everyone is asleep. I want to sleep, but I'm afraid I won't want to wake up again.
Thomas: I'll stay with you as long as you need.

ooo

"We lost each other for a while—years, really. But I always knew we'd cross paths again. There's a bond there. Sometimes thin and tenuous, sometimes even invisible, but it's always there. Somehow I understood that no matter what happened, "we" would always be in one form or another.

"And I was right. When my husband died suddenly, I was paralyzed. But then in the middle of the night, as I was scrolling through my Facebook feed, I noticed that he was online. At two a.m. I reached out to him and he reached back. He was there that night and for many nights after that, keeping me company, keeping me sane. I wouldn't have made it without him."

ooo

Three-fifteen p.m.
Becca: What are we going to do with the cat?
Thomas: The cat?
Becca: Mister, my cat? What are we going to do with him while we're away? My parents will take the kids, but my mother hates cats. And Mister doesn't care much for her either.
Thomas: Do cats enjoy cruises?
Becca: Maybe if he had his own cabin, but I refuse to take the cat on my honeymoon. He'd hog up all the attention.
Thomas: We'll figure it out.

ooo

"Thirty years. It's hard to believe I've done anything for thirty years, let alone be married. Thomas and I were meant to be together. Ah, but it went so fast. We laughed. We cried. We suffered through bad movies together.

"And now I bury another husband. The spoils of longevity are questionable at best. I had Thomas, I lost him. Then we found each other and we made a life together. Last week I lost him again. And, God willing, I will find him again someday."

Star F**ker

"You don't actually do that to guys, do you?"

A tug at my sweater stopped me just as the words, uttered in a velvety deep voice with a side of Australian, caressed my ear.

Darren McLean, heartthrob of heartthrobs. Commenting on my flirting technique, the one I learned in my high school Drama Club courtesy of a boy named Kurt who I was sure was gay but was really a woman in a man's body (he's Kathy now). I had thrown my stare at him from a cozy chair in the corner of a coffeehouse near the Hollywood Hills. I spotted him the moment he glided into the place, but kept rapt notice of the cappuccino I was nursing and the trashy novel I was pretending to read.

"Do what?" I asked, tilting my head to the right slightly, the way the teenage girls always seemed to. Playing dumb isn't my strong suit.

"That thing with your eyes. You could hurt someone with that."

"You seem fine to me."

"I'm an actor."

"Are you?" Head tilt, this time to the left.

"Darren," he said, extending his hand. When I touched it, I felt it in all the right places.

And that is when I, Jess, fell down the rabbit hole and landed in an alternate universe. I am not a lucky woman. I am not an unlucky woman either, but really amazing things seem to happen before I arrive or after I've left. But here was Darren McLean, who could melt my panties just reading a grocery list. Is he a good actor? I have no idea. Do I care? No, no I do not.

Or at least I didn't then.

In the next couple of hours I was enchanted by a charming stranger, a man who was smarter than I'd thought and more reserved than I'd been led to believe. Tabloids regularly reported tales of his sexual conquests, of women of all ages throwing themselves at him and, of course, ending up with him catching most of them. A lothario, perhaps, but more like a man who simply adores women. But the Darren sitting a foot away from me on a coffeehouse sofa was a world away from that man.

I liked this one even better.

The place closed and I expected to part ways but he took my hand and said he didn't want to be alone. A few minutes later I was on his patio, looking out over the lights of the city and fully expecting to wake up any second.

We curled up on a double chaise and picked up where we'd left off.

"What makes you happy?" he asked.

"What makes me happy? Lots of things, I guess. Big or small?"

"Small."

"Puppy breath. French vanilla ice cream. A hot bath on a cold night. *Steel Magnolias*. And probably a thousand other little things, like when the rain stops just long enough for you to get into your car."

He smiled. Wistful, not joyous.

"And you? What makes you happy?" I asked.

He looked away, out over the dark valley dotted with distant points of brilliant light. "I don't know anymore. I used to, but…"

I took his hand but said nothing. What was there to say?

He turned back to me and said, "What's your favorite song?"

Songs bled into bands, which bled into songwriters which made their way toward first loves and losing your virginity. Mine went at 18 to the first boy in college who asked. His was taken by a woman twice his age.

Who says romance is dead?

I hadn't noticed it at first, but loneliness came off of him in waves. That's what all those women responded to. They wanted to fix him. Or at least make him happy for a little while.

"When did it happen?" I said.

"When did what happen?" he said.

"When did you get broken?"

He turned toward the view again. "When I started to believe what they were saying about me."

"Who?"

"Everyone. Directors, agents, managers, reviewers…"

"What did they say?"

"That I was brilliant, the next big thing. That I was crap and getting by on my looks. That I can't act. That I can. How can one person be everything at the same time?"

I'd been brought up to believe that what other people thought of you was none of your business, but when your business is to put yourself out there, to be a public figure, I guess there was no way to avoid knowing.

I yawned.

"It's late," he said. "I'm keeping you up."

"I'm fine," I said. Then I yawned again.

"Let's go to bed."

The four loveliest words I'd ever heard. *Yes, let's.*

Darren took me by the hand and led me through the house. *Did I shave my legs? When was the last time I had a bikini wax? Am I wearing my granny panties? Oh God, what about my belly pooch? Damn I wish I'd gotten that spray tan.*

"I'm celibate," I thought I heard him say.

"I'm sorry?"

"I've gone off sex for bit. Like a detox. I was getting out of control, you know?"

"Oh, really? When?"

"Yesterday."

Naturally.

"Well. Good for you," I managed to say without a trace of sarcasm.

"I just wanted you to know that it wasn't you. You're beautiful and sexy and two days ago we'd have been in bed already."

But of course.

"Thank you." *Thank you? Thank you for not fucking me? Thank you for turning my ultimate fantasy into a flaming pile of poo?*

I slid into bed, alone, a few minutes later. I felt like crying. Once, just once something amazing was going to happen to me and then — nothing. Disappointment settled into my chest like a five-pound weight. My throat tightened. I knew the tears would come soon if I let them. And I wanted them. I deserved them. I was going to wallow in them.

And then Darren knocked on the door.

"Jess? May I come in?"

My heart leapt into my throat. "Sure." *Be cool, be cool, be cool.*

He stepped into a pool of moonlight and I could see he was wearing blue striped pajama bottoms without a shirt. And I could also see fatigue and frustration in his beautiful face.

"Would it be okay if I stayed in here?"

I pulled back the covers and patted the mattress. He got in and turned to me.

"I have a terrible time sleeping alone," he said.

I nodded and said nothing. There was nothing to say.

Then he slid closer and draped his arm over my belly, wrapped his legs around mine and nestled his head into the space between my shoulder and chin.

I was consumed by him. His smell, the feel of his skin. The weight of him on me. The rhythm of his breathing began to get slower and deeper.

I was suddenly ashamed of myself. This was a person next to me, not a movie character or poster or doll. Everyone wanted something from him; they weren't interested in Darren, they were interested in Darren McLean, whoever they thought that was.

It made me sad. Now the tears flowed. Not for me. For him.

He had the big house and the fame and the girls, but the house was empty when he came home, the fame put him on permanent display. The girls blended one into another, coming and going but never filling the empty space.

I was loved and accepted and fulfilled and missed when I was gone. I had everything.

I slept.

ooo

The scent of his cologne hit my nose seconds before his lips grazed my forehead. There are certainly worse ways to be awakened, but I don't believe there are better.

"Hi," he said, brushing a lock of hair away from my face. I died.

"Hi."

"I've got a table read in a bit, but there's still time for breakfast. Join me?"

Of course I did.

Coffee and scones and warm California sunshine. We'd come full circle to the patio. I had to leave for my flight home soon. I wondered if there was more for me here or is this all I'd get. Would I be happy with either answer?

He kissed me as I waited for a cab in front of his house. It was the kiss I'd been waiting for, one I felt from the top of my head to the bottom of my feet. If it had been the last kiss I'd ever gotten it would have been okay. At least it seemed so at the time.

"Thank you for last night. I know it probably wasn't what you expected..." he said.

"It was perfect," I said. And I meant it.

He seemed to want to say more, but cab pulled up. It was time for me to go.

And so I did.

No exchange of phone numbers or promises to be in touch.

Several months later the tabloids were all breathless and excited about Darren, his new co-star, and the baby they were expecting. A quick calculation assured me that the conception was not long after the night he'd spent curled around me, lonely and chaste.

I'm loathe to admit that I cried. A lot. It seems that for the soul-searching I'd done, the peace I believed I had made with our encounter, what I really wanted from him was no different than any of those women who'd put a hand to his knee under the table at this hotel bar or that one. The bragging rights. The great story to tell everyone who'd listen. That badge of honor.

Perhaps I'd gotten what I deserved.

Overheard In Aisle Two

They weren't looking for love, only potato chips. It was supposed to be a quick trip for both of them, just grab a bag and get home, he to the baseball game, she to one of those independent "same day as theaters" films on demand. Her steps were brisk and business-like as she rounded the corner of aisle two from one end. At the other end, he entered at a more relaxed pace. They were soon both overwhelmed at the wall of choices that confronted them. One side of the aisle, end to end, of nothing but chips. There were corn chips and pita chips and even falafel chips in addition to the stalwart potato chip. But that old favorite took up half of the shelf space. Blue potatoes, red potatoes, gold potatoes, ridged or not, kettle-cooked, gluten-free, organic, gourmet, chipotle, salsa verde, honey mustard—the choices were dizzying.

"Remember when you only had to decide between plain and sour cream and onion," she said, not looking at him.

He chuckled. "And ridges or no ridges."

She turned and smiled at him. "Exactly."

Her smile. It caught him off guard. It was electric and lit up her green eyes like a traffic light. He forgot to smile back. Her face went red and she pretended to inspect a bag of multi-colored root vegetable chips.

"It's overwhelming," he said quietly.

She nodded.

"Your smile I mean," he ventured. "It's so beautiful that it's a little overwhelming."

The smile returned, but she immediately looked down at the floor. "Thanks."

Silence took over as they both continued their quest for snacks. She thought he was cute; he thought she was gorgeous. He looked smart and had warm brown eyes. She had a mass of curly red hair and perfect, golden skin. He was embarrassed by his worn-out jeans and old Aerosmith concert t-shirt. She felt self-conscious in her once-black yoga pants and giant sweatshirt. He searched for a ring on her finger and saw none. She pretended to be engrossed in her search.

"Guys like the hot ones," he said.

"What?" She was confused and not a little insulted.

"Oh! No, no. I meant chips. Guys like the hot chips. Jalepeño, Tabasco, you know."

"I'll make a note." She turned back to the shelves. *Is he hitting on me?*, she thought. *Oh, I hope so. It's been awhile.* She continued to stare at the cornucopia of chips before her, biting the tip of her right thumb and shifting her weight from one foot to the other. After what seemed like five minutes, she peered at him out of the corner of her eye. *Go on,* she prodded herself. *Talk to him.*

"So… do you like the hot ones? Chips, of course," she said, shifting her weight to her left side and turning her head his way, but still not looking directly at him.

He thought for a moment. Searching for the right thing, the cool thing, the smooth thing to say. *What do you say to get the girl?*, he asked himself. *I have no idea*, himself responded. "No," he said finally. "I prefer the classics, like barbecue and sour cream and onion." He put his hands in his pockets. "What about you?"

"I like them plain." She shifted her weight back to her right side, closer to him. "Kinda like a blank canvas; I like to dip. You can control more of the flavor that way. And then there is the texture of the crisp chip contrasting with the creaminess of the dip. Good stuff."

He watched her eyes sparkle as she spoke. "You've given this a lot of thought, haven't you?"

"I like to live in the moment. Experience things as they come and really pay attention to them and how they make me feel. That way I know exactly what makes me happy. Do you know what makes you happy?" She looked right into his eyes.

He smiled. The smooth answer was right on the tip of his tongue. *Talking to beautiful women.* But instead he said, "Usually. But sometimes I like to surprise myself."

"Surprises are good." *That was… wow. He must think you're an idiot.* "Usually. I mean some surprises are really bad…" She stopped herself. *Make that a blathering idiot.* Her cheeks flushed bright red with embarrassment. It was all over now. She poised herself to grab a bag and make a speedy exit to the checkout.

She's nervous, he thought. *That's good, right?* Now he was nervous. And he couldn't think of a single thing to say, so he smiled. The kind of smile where your lips stay closed. The kind of smile that doesn't quite reach your eyes.

A closed-mouth smile? Oh God, he does think I'm an idiot. Now what? She took a deep breath and grabbed the first bag of chips that caught her eye. Time to make her escape. "Well," she said. "I have to go." She hesitated a second. *Stop me.*

Was she bailing on him? Now what? He grabbed a bag of his own. "Yeah. Me too." He brushed past her, heading for the checkout. *Stop me.*

"Wait," she said abruptly.

He turned toward her. Expectant. This was it.

She swallowed hard. *What do I say?* "Those are plain." *Terrific.*

"So they are," he said, looking down on the bag.

"Mine are barbecue."

They stared at each other for a beat. Then she held up her bag. "Trade ya?"

He nodded and accepted the bag from her. She took his. They smiled at each other sheepishly but said nothing.

"Have a good evening," she said when she couldn't stand the awkwardness anymore. Then she retreated down the aisle.

"You too," he called to her back.

She slowed her walk and smiled at him over her left shoulder. *Stop me.*

Stop her. His hand gave her a small wave, but he couldn't get the words out. She turned the corner and was gone.

He exchanged the barbecue chips for some plain ones and walked toward the back of the store in search of some dip.

His Name Was Joe

What shocked me most was the manner of his death, not the fact of it. I had always expected him to die young, but I'd imagined him burning out, going in a hail of gunfire or driving over a cliff. This death, it was too small for him, too quiet. A tiny little virus took him down slowly. I watched him wither; each day that larger-than-life man diminished a little more. After a few weeks I wouldn't have recognized him if we passed each other on the street even though I'd known him my whole life.

My first memory of him was at my fifth birthday party, although I imagine he'd been around before that. There was ice cream and cake and Pin-The-Tail-on-the-Donkey or some other 70s era party game. My whole Kindergarten class was there in our backyard, running and playing. I was not. I was sitting beneath the big crab apple tree that was home to the birds that I would read to after school every afternoon. I'd show them the pictures in the book just like my teacher, Miss Jones, did. But on this day I wasn't reading. I wasn't careening around the yard full of sugar and the exuberance of youth like my friends. I was pouting.

I'd opened my presents just minutes earlier and found, to my displeasure, that not one of them was the Growing Up Skipper doll I was dying for. The gifts my parents had given me earlier that day hadn't included Barbie's little sister either. What had I made my list for? I was crushed. I mumbled a thanks under my breath and stomped off to my thinking place, tucked between the folds of the tree's thick trunk. My parents tried to lure me back to the party, first by cajoling, then by threatening to send everyone home, but I was resolute. My birthday was over, a bust in spite of the bounty my mother had neatly stacked on a card table beside the kitchen door.

A commotion began with the sudden slamming of the screen door and a man's voice cutting through the laughter and joyous screaming of 15 five-year-olds.

"Uncle Joe is here!" he said so loudly that everyone stopped and turned to look. He was a stranger to me, but I quickly became interested when I noticed the box in his hand. There was no wrapping paper, only a cheap-looking green bow slapped on top of the pink box. Through the clear plastic, Growing Up Skipper smiled at me, demure in a pink and white outfit with a short gingham skirt.

He ignored everyone else and marched directly to me. Presenting the doll like it was made of solid gold, he said, "Happy Birthday, Princess."

I eagerly snatched the box from his hands and began to tear it open without a word when he leaned in.

"How 'bout a kiss for your old Uncle Joe?" He was so close I could see the pores in his nose and the web of red lines shooting through the whites of his eyes. He smelled like the beer my dad had let me take a sip of the Sunday before, yeasty and sour. I held my breath and pecked him quickly on the cheek.

"Thank you so much," I said when my nose was a safe distance. "How did you know that I wanted her?"

"A little bird told me, Princess. She wanted you to have the happiest birthday ever."

At five, I sincerely believed that one of the birds that lived in the crab apple tree sought out this man and told him my birthday wish in appreciation for all the stories I'd shared with her and her bird friends. That she chose him rather than my parents or my friends seemed significant to me. This was someone important.

That evening Daddy tucked me and Skipper into bed, kissing us both on the forehead.

"Daddy?" I said, petting the doll's blonde head absently.

"Kitten?" he said, stroking my cheek.

"Is Uncle Joe really my uncle?"

He nodded. "Yes. He's Mommy's little brother."

"Like Bobby is to me?"

"Just like that."

"How come I don't remember him?"

Daddy paused, cutting his eyes to the left and jutting out his chin. "He's been away for a while," he said finally.

"Where?"

"Upstate," he said quickly, straightening the covers. "Good night, Kitten." He kissed me again. Just before he shut the door, he whispered, "Happy Birthday."

ooo

Uncle Joe drifted in and out of our lives for a couple of years, making sporadic appearances at holidays and Sunday dinner. A few times I saw Grandma Jenny slip him some money, after which he always made a quick exit, saying he had to go to work.

The kids—me, my brother Bobby and our various cousins—adored him. When he was around he spent more time with us than with the adults. He loved to play tag or statues or any game we wanted. He always won, but we had fun anyway.

One Easter, he appeared at our house with a little gray dog asleep in his arms.

"I found this guy on the side of the road," he said. "Somebody left him there to die. Well, I wasn't about to let that happen. Why don't you all go get him some water and see if you can find something for him to eat. Maybe a little of Grandma's ham. While you're at it, get ol' Joe some too. And maybe a beer."

Later, I went into the kitchen to get more water for the pup. Grandma Jenny and Uncle Joe were standing by kitchen door whispering to each other. I couldn't hear what they were saying, and I pretended I didn't notice them so they wouldn't shoo me out. I saw Grandma take some folded bills out of her apron pocket and press them into Joe's palm.

"Thanks, Mom," he said, kissing her on the cheek. Then he was gone.

He left the dog. We named him Little Joe.

A few weeks later, Bobby and I walked out of school to find Uncle Joe waiting for us.

"No bus for you today," he said. "I'll take you home." It was a mild spring day, but he was sweating and he couldn't seem to stand still.

Bobby and I looked at each other. Why hadn't Mom told us?

"Let's go, let's go," Joe said, bouncing on the balls of his feet. He herded us into his green Nova and roared out of the parking lot—in the opposite direction of home.

"Uncle Joe, you're going the wrong way," I said.

"We're going to the park first."

"I'm hungry," Bobby said, leaning forward from the back seat.

"I have homework," I said.

"We'll get you something on the way, Cowboy," he said to Bobby. "Princess, you have to have a little fun in life. You need to learn that now, before it's too late. There'll be plenty of time for homework later."

I sat back, unconvinced. I liked getting my work done first, so I could play until dinnertime.

We stopped at a convenience store. Joe told us to wait in the car. Five minutes later he came out with two bags of Fritos, a couple of Twinkies and a can of beer in a paper bag.

"This will spoil Bobby's dinner," I said, intercepting the goodies. My five-year-old brother was a picky eater; dinner was frequently a battle of wills between him and my mother.

"Let him enjoy, Princess," Joe said, ruffling my hair. "Worry about dinner later." He plucked a bag of Fritos from my hand and passed them back. "Here you go, Cowboy."

"Thanks, Uncle Joe," Bobby said, won over by forbidden food.

I held on to the Twinkies. "You can have one of these after dinner if you clean your plate," I said to my brother.

Joe shook his head and chuckled. "Just like your mom. Now let's go!" He took a swig of his beer and peeled out of the parking lot. When we arrived he jumped out of the car and ran to the merry-go-round.

Joe grabbed the bar and ran around, getting us twirling. Then he jumped on board, grabbing Bobby and holding on tight while we squealed with pleasure. Next it was climbing on the monkey bars, followed by the swings. Joe pushed Bobby to get him started; I could take care of myself.

Once we were swinging, Joe yelled up that he would be right back. I saw him walk across the park, near the bathrooms. He shook hands with the man that had been standing there. He had a bandana on his head and was wearing a sleeveless shirt. His arms were full of tattoos. I didn't think my mother would be pleased that Uncle Joe was talking to this man; he was exactly the kind of person she had always told me to stay away from. After a couple of minutes, Joe went into the bathroom.

"I'm slowing down," Bobby said.

I brought myself to a stop so I could push him for a while until Uncle Joe came back. My arms were beginning to wear out when Joe reappeared. He'd stopped sweating and seemed more relaxed. He grabbed Bobby off of the swing.

"Time to go!" He headed toward the car.

"Aww," Bobby said. "I wanted to swing some more!"

"Sorry, Cowboy, I have my marching orders." He pulled open the car door, flipped the seat up and deposited Bobby in back.

I climbed in the passenger seat, not ready to go home myself. I checked my watch. We'd been there fifteen minutes.

Joe got in and grabbed the gear shift. Daddy had been teaching me how to work the stick shift on our car, so I wondered if Joe would let me too. I looked over at his hand on the knob.

"Do you have chicken pox?" I said, pointing to the bend in his arm, which had a bunch of red spots on it.

His whole body tightened.

"It's okay," I said. "Bobby and I have both had them."

He relaxed a bit. "I don't know. Maybe. I'll have to have that checked."

My mother was frantic when we got home. She quickly herded us into the house after inspecting us to make sure we were okay. Then she started yelling at her brother. I couldn't make out exactly what she was saying, but I heard "irresponsible" and "kidnapping" in addition to a few choice words I'd never have expected to come from my mother's mouth.

"Is Uncle Joe staying for supper?" I asked when she came back in.

"Not tonight," she said without looking at me.

We didn't see him again for a long time.

When he did reappear, we only saw him at my grandmother's house. Sometimes he was the Uncle Joe we knew and loved, sometimes he was distant and fuzzy, his eyes glassy and unfocused. But he still spent most of the time with us kids. And Grandma still slipped him cash before he'd disappear without a word. We started calling him The Phantom.

I always wondered where he went when he left us. He never talked about friends or a girlfriend or even a job. He was a mystery to me. All I knew was that when he was around, we were the center of his attention. He listened to us, he played with us. He treated us like people, and we loved him for it.

And then his appearances at family gatherings stopped suddenly. One Sunday he was there, and then we didn't see him again for months. That last Sunday he didn't play with us or even talk to us. He kicked Little Joe when he got underfoot. I got angry with him for that.

"Leave me the fuck alone," he spat at me. "Fuckin' brat."

ooo

I don't remember when Joe reappeared, but when he did, he was different. Not angry and sullen as he'd been before, but he wasn't the Uncle Joe we'd known and loved. He wore shirts that covered the tattoos on his arms and chuckled instead of laughing out loud. His big hugs were replaced by a ruffle of the hair or a pat on the head. He'd become one of the grownups. Our parents seemed happy about the change. There was a tension between the rest of the family and Joe that I hadn't even realized was there until it was gone. My mom and her other siblings, along with Grandma Jenny, seemed softer, more relaxed than I'd ever known them to be. And so we settled into this new normal.

ooo

When I was 14, Little Joe died. He'd had a good life with us, but he was old and tired. One night we went to bed and the next morning he didn't come when I called. He was curled up on his bed. I petted his head. He was ice cold.

I was inconsolable.

He was more than a dog to me. He was the embodiment of everything I wanted to be then: joyful and free with so much love to give. He was Uncle Joe before he "grew up" as my parents said. Now I was all alone.

"There'll be other dogs," my mother said as she held me tight. It was meant to comfort me.

I didn't want another dog. I wanted Joe back.

My grief stretched from days to weeks to a month with no end in sight. I thought I would never be happy again.

I was staring out the window of my room into the tree-lined street in front of our house when that familiar green Nova roared up to the curb. My heart leapt.

The man that moved up the walkway had a bounce in his step, an exuberance I'd thought I'd never see again. My Uncle Joe was back.

Moments later he was in my bedroom, hands in his pockets, looking at me with his head tilted.

"When did you get so grown, Princess?"

I blushed and smiled.

"I'm sorry about Little Joe," he said. "But I don't think he'd want you sitting around missing him like this. He'd want you to go out and have fun."

I looked out the window again. The sun was shining, the air was warm. It was a beautiful day, just the kind of day Little Joe would have spent running around the backyard, splashing in the blow-up pool I'd bought for him with my allowance. "You think?" I asked.

"I know."

I nodded. "Okay."

We headed out the door. "Should I get Bobby?" I said.

Joe thought for a moment, then shook his head. "This one's just for you."

We drove out of town and into the country. He turned onto an old dirt road, and stopped the car.

"Wanna drive?" he asked, eyebrows raised.

I did. But I was only 14. "Hell yes," I said.

He vacated the driver's seat and I took his place. He helped me adjust the seat and then said, "Let's do this."

It was an exhilarating ride. A little slow at first, but as my confidence grew, so did our speed. Joe whooped and hollered and cheered me on. I drove up and down that dirt road twenty or thirty times that day. I couldn't wait to tell all of my friends.

On the way back to town, Joe said, "This is between you and me, Princess. Your mom would be pissed if she found out and we'd never be able to do it again. Promise me you'll keep this between us."

We pinky swore.

We stopped at 7-Eleven on the way home to get a couple of cold ones (beer for him, soda for me) to celebrate. While Joe paid I walked back to the Nova.

From my left I heard a low whistle. "Hey little mama, looking good. Why don't you come over here so I can get a better look at you?"

There was no one else around, so I knew he was talking to me. I didn't know what to do, so I ignored him.

"Hey, I'm talking to you, bitch. You think you're better than me?"

I walked a little faster, my face hot and my throat tightening. Then I heard footsteps coming up behind me.

"I said I'm talking to you, bitch. Didn't anyone teach you any…"

"Hey!" It was Uncle Joe. "She's 14, asshole. Leave her alone."

"She's old enough to have some manners," the guy shot back.

I turned around to see Joe grabbing him by the neck. "You're the one with the bad manners, pal. Now back off and leave her alone."

"I see how it is," the guy said, retreating. "You're keeping her for yourself."

Joe, who had started walking toward the car, whirled around said, "What did you say?" Without waiting for an answer, he began running toward the guy.

"Joe!" I screamed. Something bad was about to happen. "Let's go. I have to get home before mom does."

That stopped him. He turned and walked back to the car and drove me home.

ooo

"Tom, he's my brother. I can't just leave him there," my mom said.

It was late. My parents thought I was asleep. But I couldn't stop thinking about that afternoon. The look on that guy's face. His voice. The look on Joe's face. The rage I felt coming from him. I'd never felt that before.

"If he's using again he might be better off," my dad said.

My mom sighed. "Please."

I couldn't hear any more. And I wouldn't see Joe again for several years. My parents told me he got a job upstate. I wondered why he didn't even send me a card on my birthday.

"He's busy, I guess," said my mom on my 16th birthday.

ooo

"Princess?" I heard behind me. I turned. It was a man with graying hair. Reed thin. Pale, blotchy skin. Too pale.

"Joe?" It didn't look like him, but no one had called me that in the 10 years since I'd last seen him.

He nodded. I smiled and hugged him. He felt so small.

"Where have you been? How have you been?" I said.

"Come on," he said, taking my hand and leading me into the corner diner. We sat and ordered. Coffee for me, hot tea for Joe.

He took both my hands in his. "I guess they didn't tell you," he began. He laughed. "I wouldn't have either.

"I've been in prison."

"Upstate," I said.

He nodded. "Remember that day I took you driving?"

I nodded.

"And that guy…"

"Yes," I said, taking back my hands, remembering his rage, not wanting to hear what was next.

He looked out the window. Fussed with his tea bag. "I went back to the store after I dropped you off. He was still there. I beat him until my hands were bloody, until my shirt was bloody. I beat him until he stopped moving."

"Did you…"

"No, I didn't kill him. But he was in the hospital for a long time. I just got out recently."

I was equally honored and disgusted. "I don't know what to say."

"There's nothing to say. I was high. I'd been clean for almost a decade, but I slipped. I slipped hard. I was high when I came to get you."

"And now?"

"I've been clean ever since. But things have a way of catching up to you."

"What do you mean?"

"I have AIDS," he said simply.

I shook my head. "How?"

"Remember the chicken pox on my arm? Track marks. I used to shoot heroin. I shared needles."

ooo

The rest is hospitals and that peculiar disinfectant smell. The longer he was there, the bigger the bed got. His eyes sank back into this head. I held his hand as he slipped away. I was the only one there. Grandma Jenny had passed away a few years ago. My mother wanted nothing to do with him. Neither did the rest of the family. He was the black mark on our name. The secret we didn't tell people. But I chose to remember the times he made me laugh, the times when he made me feel special and important, like I mattered. And I returned the favor.

The Last Bottle
of Scotch

Early evening. Manhattan. Twenty-first floor. The lights are low, the skyline coming to life beyond the floor-to-ceiling windows as day gives way to night. Candles flicker in the center of small, round dining table where a middle-aged couple are seated. On the radio, Al Martino is singing "I Love You More Every Day."

"Is this from that place around the corner?" he asks, pushing Veal Francaise around on the plate. Making a show of eating.

"San Marino, yes," she answers, making her own show. "Best in the city."

"Hmm."

Silence.

"How was your day?" she asks.

"Long," he says. "Yours?"

"Long." Pause. "Would you like some more salad?"

"No." Pause. "Thank you."

"I read in the paper that Elizabeth Taylor and Eddie Fisher got divorced."

"What's that, her fifth?"

"Fourth, I think. Such a shame, isn't it? You'd think such a beautiful woman…"

"It is." He reaches for the heavy-bottomed old-fashioned glass in front of him. Wedding gift. Best one they'd gotten. He drains the amber liquid inside. Its warmth wends its way down his throat and into his belly. His shoulders are beginning to relax. "But you never know what's going on in other people's marriages."

"No, you don't, do you?" she says.

"Did you see that Jimmy Hoffa got convicted? I would have loved to have worked on that case."

"I bet you would have won it," she says, smiling.

"Win or lose, it would have been a great case. Career-making."

"It'll happen." She reaches over and pats his hand.

He picks up the bottle of Johnnie Walker Double Black sitting between them. He pours two fingers and returns it to its spot on the table.

"One more left," she says idly. She still has a few sips in her glass, but the ice is melting. She turns to the bar sink behind her and dumps the watered-down scotch, along with the ice. She grabs three ice cubes from the well-used bucket on the counter. Another wedding gift. *Clink, clink, clink.* In they go. She loves that sound.

"Is there another bottle in there?" He asks. Trying to be casual.

She checks the black lacquered cabinet, which usually houses several. "No," she says, surprised. "That's the last one." Her throat goes tight. She reaches for the fifth on the table.

"Wait. We'll split it."

"You just poured a fresh one. This is mine."

"Arlene." Panic.

She sits back, crosses her arms and glares at him. "What?"

"You don't really need that, do you? You've had a few already…"

"That bottle was full when we sat down," she snaps. "You've had just as much as I have. More, since you just filled your glass. The rest is mine."

He sighs. "Call downstairs and have Jeffrey run to the liquor store and get a couple more bottles."

"It's Sunday."

"So?"

"The liquor store is closed."

He looks down at his still-full plate. "Didn't you notice we were low?"

"There were three bottles there when I went out yesterday afternoon."

He glares at her. She fidgets. Uncomfortable. Guilty.

"I thought that we might go out last night so…," she says.

"Saturday night *Bonanza* is on TV. Besides, I told you I was tired."

"You did." She taps her fork around her own still-full plate.

More silence. Thicker this time.

Arlene shifts in her seat. Derek holds on to his glass for dear life. Neither takes their eyes off of the bottle.

"Um… speaking of shopping, I'll need some money for the groceries this week," she says.

"What about your house allowance? It's only the beginning of the month. Don't you have anything left?"

"I…"

"Check your wallet. Isn't there anything in there?"

"Just my five-year chip," she says, looking directly at him.

"That's worthless , isn't it?"

"It is now." She picks up her glass, looks inside, then puts it down again.

"Guilt is a terrible thing."

"Yes, Derek, it is. So is trying to be sober around a drunk who looks more lovingly at a bottle of Dewar's than at you." She turns behind her again and opens a silver box, pulls out a cigarette. She taps it on the top of the cabinet. *Tap, tap, tap.*

Hands on the table, leaning in. "So it was my fault?" *It was true. Sometimes.*

"Yes. No," she says. She lights the cigarette and blows out a column of smoke. "You were the reason, but it's my own fault. I chose."

"What was his name again?"

"Sam." *Samantha.*

Derek smiles. A crocodile smile. "But I won in the end, didn't I?"

"No," she says. Sad. "I lost. My integrity. Once that was gone, it was so easy to crawl back into the bottle. You didn't win, Johnnie Walker did."

He takes another sip from his glass. Eyes the bottle. "Sure you don't have another bottle somewhere? You were always like a little squirrel, building a little stash just in case."

"No." She closes her eyes.

A beat. Two.

"There's chocolate cake for dessert," she says finally.

"I'd have rather had the scotch."

"Me too," she sighs, takes one last drag of her cigarette then grinds it out in the ashtray.

Scotch is all they drink. And a lot of it.

"When we met you only drank wine or fruity drinks. I had to give you an education," he says. Attempting playful. Sounding accusatory.

"You were a pretentious poser trying to look more sophisticated by drinking single malt," she says. Pauses. "I really didn't like you."

"What changed your mind?"

"You wore me down. And once you stopped handing me tired lines and started to actually talk to me like a person, I discovered that you were not nearly as big an ass as you appeared to be."

He nods, but says nothing. He's a defense lawyer who represents scumbag criminals. He is an even bigger ass than she'd thought.

They sit in silence. A long, heavy silence, the kind that makes you fidget and strain for something to say. Instead they both keep an eye on the bottle and push the food around their plates some more. "I Want To Hold Your Hand" comes on the radio.

"Turn that teenybopper crap off," Derek says, tossing his napkin on the table.

She does. "I like it."

"You would."

"A long time ago you would have too."

"Do you remember why you fell in love with me? " he asks her, leaning forward. Was there anything left of that guy? She leans forward as well, poised to lunge across the table and grab the bottle if he even so much as twitches a hand toward it.

"No," she replies. Lying. He'd been funny, sweet, ambitious. He made her feel like more than she was.

"Me either," he says, sitting back. He leans toward her again and asks, "Do you love me now?"

"I don't think so." Maybe a little true.

"Did you ever really?" *I was worth loving once, before I sold my soul.*

"I must have or I wouldn't be here," she says. "I certainly didn't marry you for your money." One eye on the scotch.

"I wouldn't have married you if that's what you were after. There are a lot of flaws I can tolerate, but stupidity is not one of them." They were broke back then.

"You don't think I'm stupid? Look where I am, look what I'm doing. If this isn't stupid, I don't know what is."

"You're drunk." Accusing. Changing the subject.

"Of course I am. It's the only way I can stay in this marriage. I think it's how you got me to marry you in the first place." A pause. She softens. "Remember our wedding? Remember how I snuck that flask in the dressing room tucked into my little blue garter?" She smiles. "My mother and sisters had no idea. I kept fiddling with my gown, but they never caught on. God, it was the only way I could survive in there with Mother nattering at me, telling me I should have gone on a diet before the wedding, I should have dyed my hair a different color, I should have bought a different dress…"

"You should have been a different person," he says, laughing.

Arlene laughs too. Bitter. Because it was true. She should have been someone else. She stares out the window at the city. He stares at her, wondering what happened to them.

"I called you Friday afternoon—why didn't you answer? You couldn't have been busy." He didn't know what she did all day; he hadn't asked in a long time.

"I didn't answer because I didn't want to talk to anyone. What did you want?"

Absolution. "I got chewed out about some case I allegedly didn't file. I needed my wife to give me a pep talk." A lie.

"Have you met your wife? I don't do pep talks. Did you forget to file the case or not?"

"I don't know." He didn't forget to file a case.

"You don't know? Why don't you know?"

"I don't remember anything about that afternoon." That was the story he was going to stick with.

"Your first blackout. Congratulations." She laughs. Hollow.

There was no blackout. He remembers every second of that afternoon. He called because he discovered that a witness who was about to testify against his client was found dead. "No. I was very busy that day. People to talk to about this case I'm in the middle of. Preparing for trial."

"You weren't drunk?"

He is never drunk anymore, not like in the beginning. He drinks to stay even. He shakes his head. "I was interviewing a witness…" They stare at each other. More silence. He gulps the last of the booze in his glass, then sets it down on the table. He runs his right hand through his hair, then picks up his fork and idly twirls some bucatini onto it.

"How did you know you'd hit bottom?" he asks, still looking at the pasta-filled fork. He thinks he might be there now. Or maybe he was when he handed the envelope to his client's "associate," a guy, truth be told, who looked exactly like you would expect a murderer to look. *Just some things that I need him to take care of, Derek,* the client, a shady character himself, had said.

"I couldn't see a way out anymore," she says quietly.

"Why'd you start drinking again?"

She sighs. "I couldn't see a way out anymore."

"Out of what? The affair? The marriage?"

Looking at the table. "What I'd made of my life."

She wonders what her new bottom will be. She knows it is coming, and anticipates it eagerly, almost willing it along by drinking a little more every day, regardless of how ill she feels in the morning—half the day, really.

"Should I leave you?" she asks him.

"Probably," he replies. "But I wish you wouldn't." *I won't survive without you; I need help.* He should tell her, but can't.

"Why?" *Give me a reason to stay.*

"Who would I drink with at night?" He gives her a weak smile, gets nothing. It was true. His friends, his drinking buddies, don't answer his calls anymore.

"Don't you want your life back?" *Please.*

Yes. "This is my life."

"It will kill you."

"Yes. It will," he says quietly. *It might be better that way.*

"You would leave me all alone?"

"You could come with me." *Save me.*

She shakes her head. "I don't want to die. And I want a real life. A normal life."

"A boring life." He stares up at the ceiling. *Is it? Boring?*

She sits up in her chair and spreads her arms wide. "You don't think this is boring? Sitting around hammered all the time? When was the last time you actually did anything?"

He shakes his head. "Dunno. You?"

"I'm not sure." She sinks back into her chair.

"Maybe when you were fucking Sam," he says matter-of-factly.

"Probably." Absently. She misses Sam.

He nods, leans back in his chair. Angry now. She betrayed him. Scotch never has. Not that he would admit.

"You gonna drink that?" he asks, nodding toward the Johnnie Walker.

She considers for a moment, then shakes her head. "No."

He reaches for the neck of the bottle.

"Don't," she says, extending her hand as if to grab it away.

He ignores her and pours the last of the liquid into his empty glass.

"You don't want that," she says. "Pour it down the sink." She wants it, but she doesn't want to want it.

"You don't know what I want." *I don't know what I want.*

She considers him for a moment. "You're right. I have no idea what you want." Resigned. "Tell me."

"I want you to leave me alone to drink this in peace." He wants not to have to choose. Not right now.

"And then what?"

"Then I want to go pass out so I can start all over again tomorrow." *I want to sleep and sleep then wake up and all of this was a dream.*

She nods. "Okay."

"Okay?"

She nods again. "Okay."

"What does that mean?" He sets the glass down on the table.

"It means okay. Do what you want. Live the way you want to live. But I won't stand around and watch you kill yourself. This stops right here for me. When you wake up, I'll be gone."

If she leaves him, he'll be lost. But this isn't the first time she's threatened. He looks at her, then back at the scotch. Pretending to choose.

"There's a meeting close by in the morning if you want to join me," she says. Testing.

He stands up, gulps down his drink, then sets the glass down on the table, hard. "No thanks," he says. "I'm good." He disappears into the bedroom.

Arlene gets up and stacks the dirty dishes together in a pile. She considers taking them into the kitchen, but changes her mind. She packs up the empty food containers and the empty bottle and throws them in the trash. She checks the bedroom; Derek is already snoring, in that way only real drunks do.

She hurries into the living room and to the bookcase, which is packed with books they'd read. When they'd read. She hasn't picked one up in more than six months; Derek even longer. She reaches behind a teetering pile, pulls out a full bottle of Dewar's and brings it into the dining room. She sits down and places it in front of her.

Stares at it for a moment. Open or not? Open, she thinks, reaching for it. Her hand stops halfway. Instead she pulls a notebook from her purse, and quickly scribbles something.

When Derek shuffles out the next morning, he sees the scotch and thinks his day has just gotten better. Then he notices the note.

I hope you two have a very happy life together. —Arlene

Her house keys are looped around the neck of the bottle.

A Month of Sundays

She opened one eye and looked out the bedroom window. Fat clouds had settled in and pushed closer to the ground, painting the sky a flat gray that would linger for months. She wanted to stay in bed. Pull the covers over her face and disappear into dreams. But it was Sunday, and David was waiting.

Any other day she'd be turned out, well dressed, a chic urban woman. But Sundays were for sweats and thick socks, her hair piled on top of her head in a messy ponytail, her face scrubbed and bare. Her slippers scraped the sidewalk as she made her rounds.

At the newsstand she hefted *The New York Times* on the counter with a thud, her money on top. She smiled at the man behind the counter. A weary smile. But she always smiled at him. He smiled back, as he did every Sunday.

The newspaper weighed down the battered canvas tote, the one she always used. She stopped at the bakery. Three large croissants—two plain, one chocolate—added their weight to the bag. Already tucked inside, next to the *Times*, was a large thermos of coffee. She noticed the heaviness of it all, how the straps dug into her shoulder—had they always done that? She stopped, shifted the load, took a deep breath. David was waiting.

It was a Saturday, that first night they'd spent together. His place. Too wired to sleep, she'd watched him dream until weak morning light seeped in around the edges of the blinds, then slipped out quietly to explore the neighborhood. She returned an hour later with still-warm pastries, hot coffee, and the monstrous newspaper.

"What's this?" David asked.

"Sunday," she said.

They sat on the floor in the living room, picking and sipping, reading quietly and aloud to each other, every page, starting with the Arts section. Attempting the crossword but leaving it unfinished, cast aside in a fit of feigned frustration that ended in giggly sex. That was Sunday.

The drive had become as familiar as her own face, and she often didn't remember any of it. Get in the car, start it, and suddenly there she was. But today she noticed that the leaves on the towering trees, once resplendent in hues of red and orange, were mottled, brown and dry, letting go, falling away. The tree trunks looked black and gnarled, the sky was cold steel. She pined for the warmth and safety of her bed, and fought the urge to turn back and let it overtake her. David was waiting.

She trudged across the brown grass, in between the headstones, the heft of her tote and the thick blanket she carried making both her steps and her breathing labored. When she reached the big oak tree she sighed with relief and set her burdens down.

She approached the tall gray marker slowly, as if it were an altar. On its flat top were three small stones in the same charcoal hue, their shiny finish in contrast with the matte surface of the headstone. She reached in her pocket and pulled out an identical one. For a moment she regarded the rock in her open hand, then returned it to her pocket. From the bag she pulled her wallet and eased out a small, flat blue stone. David had nicked it from a bowl filled with them at the entrance to a restaurant on their first date.

"It matches your eyes," he'd said.

She placed it beside the others, then touched each of them lightly with a single finger as if playing a scale: pinky, ring, middle, index.

She'd seen Jewish families put rocks on the graves of their loved ones. A small gesture that said someone was there, that the person beneath this patch of earth is loved, is missed. David was loved. And missed.

Each Sunday since he died she'd brought another polished stone. Every week she ate too many croissants, read the entire Sunday *Times*, and failed to finish the crossword. Soon she wouldn't be able sit on the frozen ground for hours. *If only he'd died in the summer*, she thought. Spring would return the leaves to the trees and the green to the grass, but where would she be? Now is all she had.

So now she laid down the heavy blanket, arranged the newspaper, set out the pastries, and poured the coffee.

"Shall we start with the Arts section?" she said.

Surrender, Dorothy

"Dorothy, I want to become a woman," Michael said to me at breakfast that morning, a stack of four perfect, golden brown pancakes, dripping with butter and syrup, in front of him. He was holding his knife in one hand and his fork in the other, wrists resting lightly on the table as he spoke, as if he aimed to perform the deed right then.

I laughed. It was a joke, my strong, masculine Michael, the man who had fucked me silly a half an hour ago, a woman? It had to be a joke so I laughed. But he didn't laugh back. He nodded his head and looked directly into my eyes and didn't even smile.

Wait. It didn't actually happen that way. That's the way it felt at the time. The truth is he didn't fuck me silly that morning. We had sex. Sort of. Really it was just that he… Well, it was all about me. The sex was never all that good. I just didn't know the difference back then. The rest of it happened pretty much that way. I was blindsided.

"Why?" It was the only word I could summon the breath to push out of my throat, the most important word in the world at that moment. "Why?"

"It's who I am. Who I've always been. It's time for me to be who I am and not what I turned out to be."

No. Michael was my husband, a man. We'd be married a year in August. Happily married. Blissfully married. Man and woman, husband and wife. That was what he promised, the question he asked on that technicolor day in May when the tulips were blooming in the park and we were on our backs on a blanket, staring up at a brilliant blue sky. A small plane flew overhead pulling a yellow banner that said, "Surrender, Dorothy." My favorite movie is *The Wizard of Oz*. It was his way of asking me to spend my life with him. He wrapped his arms around me and whispered it in my ear. "Surrender, Dorothy," he said. And I did.

"No," I said. "You're a man. That's what you are. You're a man and I'm a woman." I made this simple declaration and returned to my own, smaller stack of pancakes. The discussion was closed.

"Yes," he said as he stood. "I will become a woman, with you or without you." He washed his dish and put it in the drainer before he walked into the bedroom. "Thank you for breakfast," he said, touching my cheek gently as he passed by.

I stared at his empty chair for an hour before I was able to move.

We'd been seniors in high school when we first discovered each other. We'd grown up together, been in the same Kindergarten class, made the rounds to the same chaotic, sugar-loaded birthday par- ties each year. Mickey was the brown-haired boy who was the pack leader, the one the other boys looked to and followed. He was a part of the fabric of my life, but he remained in the background, just someone I knew. He'd signed three of my yearbooks with a simple "Take Care" and his name, the same way he'd signed everyone else's. It was all very friendly but superficial. And then one day it wasn't. One day he looked at me and I noticed how beautiful his smile was, how white his teeth were. I noticed that over the summer he'd grown taller and more muscular and that my stomach fluttered a bit when- ever he looked my way. He noticed me too. Maybe that was what I noticed the most. That he saw me. Other boys didn't. At least not yet. But Michael did, and I liked it.

He was different from the other boys, too, sweet and gentle. He never pushed me for sex. Ever. That should have been my first clue, but it was a relief to me, a departure from a home life where I had to lock the door at night to keep my stepfather out. Michael was exactly what my battered psyche needed. We were perfect together.

I sat remembering that beautiful, wonderful boy and our first kiss and the slight roughness of his hands as he cupped my face, and I cried. I cried until there wasn't a drop of moisture left in my body. I cried until the muscles in my stomach were so sore I couldn't sit upright. I cried until the kitchen filled with shadows and my husband came home.

He cleared the table and did the dishes while I stayed at the table, my mind far away.

"I'm me. I'll always be me. I'll just look different." He crouched down beside my chair, took my hand and kissed it.

"How will I know it's you? You'll look different and probably smell different and feel different."

"Your heart will know," he said.

Later, we curled around each other in the dim early-evening light of our bedroom. It all felt so familiar, so normal and yet so completely altered.

"Michael?" I whispered.

"Yes," he said into my hair.

"What am I going to call you? What is your name going to be when… you know." I couldn't say, "when you are a woman." I almost couldn't even think it, but there were so many questions in my head I had to catch them and ask them as I could.

"Michaela. So it's not so different."

"Can I call you Mickey? They call girls Mickey, don't they?" I called him Mickey sometimes. It's what his mother used to call him.

"Would that make you happy?"

"Not happy. What would make me happy is for everything to stay the way it is, for you to be my husband. For us to share this bed forever."

He pulled up on his elbow and looked down into my eyes. "Just because I'll be a woman won't mean that I don't want to be with you. I love you. I always have and I always will. This won't change that."

"It changes everything; you'll be a woman. We won't be man and wife, we'll be woman and…"

"You'll always be my wife. The outside stuff is just physical."

"I like men."

Did I? Because the extent of my experience was my sweaty, smelly stepfather and a man who didn't believe he was supposed to be a man.

He sat up straight. "So you won't stay with me if I'm not a man?"

"I don't know," I said. "I just don't know."

He turned to roll over and shut me out, but I stopped him by grabbing his arm. "No. You can't just turn off because you don't like what you hear. I could have walked out that door hours ago and never looked back, but I'm here. I need to make sense of this."

There's no way I could have walked out on him then. I had nowhere to go, no way to support myself. I kept telling myself that I loved him and wanted to give him a chance when I really just had no other option. I stayed because I had to.

"How long have you known this is what you wanted?"

He pulled away from my grasp. "It's not what I *want*, it's what I *am*."

"Fine. How long have you known?"

"For as long as I can remember."

I sat up. "I've known for about four hours. You think you can give me a little time to get used this and figure out how I feel? Because, honestly, this information would have been very helpful before you asked me to marry you. You knew and didn't share that with me; I didn't have all the information I needed to make a choice. You did. I'm going to have trouble with this; I will try my best for you though because I love you."

He nodded. "OK," he said. I could see the tears shining in his eyes in the dim light. "I'm sorry. About everything." He lay down, put his arms around me and tucked his face into the curve of my neck. "For a long time I didn't know what I was feeling. Once I did, it got worse, not better. I couldn't tell anyone. Then I met you and I thought that maybe it was just a phase; how could I be a girl inside and be in love with a girl? After a while that didn't matter anymore; I knew who I was. But I didn't know how to tell you. Or anybody. I was afraid I'd lose you."

"I know."

"I still am."

"I know."

"I don't know if I can make it without you. You are my world. You're my best friend, the other half of my soul."

I was angry. I felt betrayed. I loved him and would stand by him for as long as I could, but in the deepest part of my soul I felt that I couldn't stay with him as Michaela. And in another part I held onto the hope that he would change his mind if he thought that he would lose me, that our love was more powerful than whatever was driving his desire to change.

I was wrong. Within two days he came home with a copy of *The Transgender Companion* and joined a support group for transgender people. This was real. It was happening. He started seeing a psychologist. A few weeks later he came home and told me he'd made an appointment with a doctor to get female hormones. And then it was far too real.

I didn't go with him to the doctor, although he'd asked me to. I considered it, but I thought it would seem as if I was okay with it. I wasn't, so he went alone. I made sure I wasn't home when he got back.

I was so sheltered I didn't even know that being transgender was a real thing. The only men trying to be women I'd ever experienced was on TV sitcoms. I had no idea what to expect. I think I just assumed it would be Michael in a dress. I was totally unprepared for what was coming.

Over the next few months, the distance between us grew wider as the features of his face began to soften and he began to change. Each step he took toward his destination was one step farther from me, from us. The man I adored was blurring at the edges, fading into a creature I neither knew nor really cared to know. We still shared a bed but I had moved out of "our" space and into my own after I'd moved to wrap my legs around his in the middle of the night and discovered they'd been shaved.

The worst part about all of this was that I carried the burden of Michael's transformation alone. His parents had died just after we'd graduated high school, and he had no brothers or sisters and no contact with distant relatives. There was no one to commiserate with, no one to vent to. This particular brand of hell was a solitary one; even if others knew, could they truly understand how I felt? I cried a lot, alone in my room when Michael was gone. Sometimes I drew a hot bath and sat in the tub, the sounds of my sobs covered by the rush of the water and my red face explained by the steam. My husband was leaving me, and I felt like the person who held me up when I couldn't stand on my own, the one who was my rock, my best friend, was leaving with him.

Night was the worst. In the haze between sleep and wakefulness, I'd forget and try to curl up in his arms. But instead of hard muscle in his belly, arms and back, he felt softer.

I waited for a couple of weeks. Then I moved to the couch.

"You should go to counseling," he said. "You really should think about it. It'll help you deal with this, to work through your feelings. To understand it."

"I don't want to understand it. I don't want to deal with it. I want my fucking life back, Mike. I want my husband. I wanna have kids. I don't want to be a lesbian; I can't change who I am."

"Neither can I," he said.

We were on opposite sides of a deep gorge that neither of us was brave enough to jump.

There were good moments, of course. Whole days even when it felt like we were us again. If I closed my eyes so I couldn't see how round his face had gotten and if I ignored the way his voice had changed, I could fool myself into thinking it was going to be OK. I still had the best parts of my husband, his sense of humor, his tenderness and his love, but all it took was a glimpse of polished toenail, the new smoothness of his skin, and I remembered that my husband wasn't there anymore.

ooo

"And that's how I ended up here," I said.

I was in the office of Taylor Morgan, Ph.D, perched on the black leather couch, which was a little cold on the backs of my bare thighs. Why had I worn shorts? My mother taught me that a lady dressed up for certain occasions and I was pretty sure this would qualify as one of them. It was sort of an act of defiance, my way of saying this wasn't all that important to me, that this was an empty gesture designed so that I could say I tried.

Dr. Morgan unfolded her arms and rested them on her thighs, leaning forward and looking me straight in the eye. "Sounds like you have a problem," she said gently.

That's when I started to cry.

ooo

"I've been coming here for months. Why can't I make any sense of this yet?" I whined to Dr. Morgan one autumn afternoon.

"I'm not sure you have to make any sense of it," she said. "In the end you have to accept it, then you have to either accept or reject the idea of a romantic relationship with Michaela." She always called Michael by his girl's name. I still thought of him as Michael. I couldn't even bring myself to say, 'Michaela,' even in my head. "Do you feel like you are getting anything out of our sessions?"

I nodded. "I don't feel so alone anymore." It helped me cope with watching my husband fade into a woman that I didn't recognize, one who spoke like the love of my life and had his laugh.

"Are you still sleeping on the couch?"

"Yeah. I go through the motions of being supportive, but it's bullshit. I'm keeping him at arm's length even though I miss him terribly. All I want to do is talk to my best friend about it. Except he's my best friend. He used to be anyway." I felt we were on opposite sides of a tall chain-link fence: We could see each other, but we couldn't reach each other without a climb, which, at any given time, one or the other of us didn't seem willing or able to make.

"Do you have any idea what Michaela is going through right now? Can you even imagine?" she asked.

I shook my head.

"Maybe it's time you tried to find out."

ooo

I began reading a lot. Books by other women who'd been through the same thing I was going though. Books by women who'd been born men. I hoped that in those pages I'd find a way through this. Some days I felt I was making progress, that maybe it would be okay. Other days I felt just as hopeless and alone as ever. Those were days I tried to stay away from Michael so I wouldn't hurt his feelings. On his way to womanhood, he'd become a bit fragile. Some of that, of course, was my fault. Rejection is never easy.

I think that was it, what was at the bottom of what I was feeling, underneath all the confusion. I felt rejected by Michael. I'd thought we had a nice life, but he wanted to change everything.

A few weeks later, I was having one of my bad days. They were fewer and farther between, interrupted with periods of numbness. But that day was all angry tears. And then Michael walked in the door wearing a blouse that I would have picked out for myself. It was a fitted indigo button-down that accentuated his broad shoulders. He left the top two buttons opened, revealing a waxed chest and a vintage silver necklace that I would have killed for. The shirt was tucked into a pair of simple gray trousers. It was beautiful and classic.

I sobbed and bolted from the living room. He waited for a few minutes, then knocked on the bedroom door.

"Go away," I said. He opened the door anyway and sat down next to me on the bed.

"I know that as hard as this is for me, it's a hundred times harder for you," he said. "I still feel the same way about you that I've always felt, but I know you don't. I'm terrified that I am going to lose you. You're my life."

He put his arms around me. I smelled flowery perfume and hairspray. The way he held me was different, gentler. As I put my arms around him, I noticed once again that he felt softer and rounder. I buried my nose in his neck the way I had a hundred times before. I didn't recognize the smell of his skin anymore.

I moved out the next day.

I moved back in a week later.

One week on a friend's couch was five days too many. I missed my things and my own bed. And, strangely, I missed Michael, although at the time I couldn't even admit it to myself. I just told him that I had reconsidered and felt that I shouldn't have to leave my home.

I asked him to move out.

"This is my home too," he said. "I don't want to leave."

I didn't respond.

"Dorothy, please."

I shrugged my shoulders and went back to unpacking. I never mentioned it again. What could I say? And while there was a tightness in my stomach when we were together, there was a hole there when we were apart.

"This must be why people kill themselves," I said to Dr. Morgan a few days later. "Neither option is appealing. But right now the hole is much scarier."

"Do you feel like you want to hurt yourself?" There was concern in her voice, not her usual neutral tone.

I shifted in my seat. I cocked my head to the side and looked up to the ceiling for the answer. "I don't think so," I said finally.

She let out the breath she'd been holding. "You're not sure?"

"I don't want to die," I said. "I just can't face the hole."

"Tell me about the hole."

"My father died when I was six. Mom didn't do very well on her own, so by the time I was seven she'd married again. Lee. My stepfather." I closed my eyes and took a deep breath. "It wasn't long after they got married that…" I squirmed in my seat, unable to get comfortable. "That Lee started coming into my room at night."

Dr. Morgan was silent, waiting for me to finish. I shook my head. I couldn't.

"He wasn't just tucking you in," she said. A statement, not a question.

"No. He wasn't."

"And the hole?"

"It's been there ever since. Or it was until Michael."

"Did your mother…"

"I don't know what she knew, but I believe she'd have picked him over me. She needed a man. And I guess I do too, don't I?

"I felt right with Michael, like I was okay and nothing bad could touch me anymore. He helped me put a lock on my bedroom door. He gave me the courage to fight back."

"And without him?" she asked.

"I feel like that girl, lying in bed, waiting for the bad thing to come."

ooo

A year after we'd sat in the kitchen, eating pancakes, me basking in afterglow, Michael tearing a hole in the fragile fabric of our union, and we seemed no closer to being more than roommates, but we'd settled into an unspoken détente.

I was ignoring it. Getting on with my life, doing what I needed to do. So was Michael. It was as if the past year never happened. Except that instead of a husband, I lived with a six-foot girl who wore size 12 pumps and dressed better than I did.

I had just come home from the laundromat and went into the bedroom to put the clean clothes away. I dropped the basket on the bed and began transferring socks and underwear to their homes in the dresser Michael and I still shared. Several times I almost put his panties in my drawer when I remembered that he preferred the lacy bikinis while I leaned toward cotton boy shorts, which made me laugh. When I laughed, I realized that I hadn't in quite a while.

I picked up a stack of towels and headed for the linen closet next to the bathroom. I was burying my nose in the soft terry and inhaling the scent of lavender when I saw Michael sitting at the bathroom counter. He was inches from the mirror, mouth in an O, one eye open, the other closed with what appeared to be a spider crawling on it. He was putting on false eyelashes. Or trying to. I watched him struggle for a few minutes, his frustration mounting until I thought I saw tears well in his eyes. I felt a familiar fullness in my chest, an ache I'd almost forgotten. I walked into the bathroom and set the towels down on the counter.

"Here," I said. "Let me help."

Mickey sat still while I applied a fringe of dark black lashes to each eye. When I'd finished, we both looked in the mirror, contemplating the results.

"Thank you," she said, with a shy smile.

I smiled back.

"I love you," she said tentatively.

"I love you, too," I said.

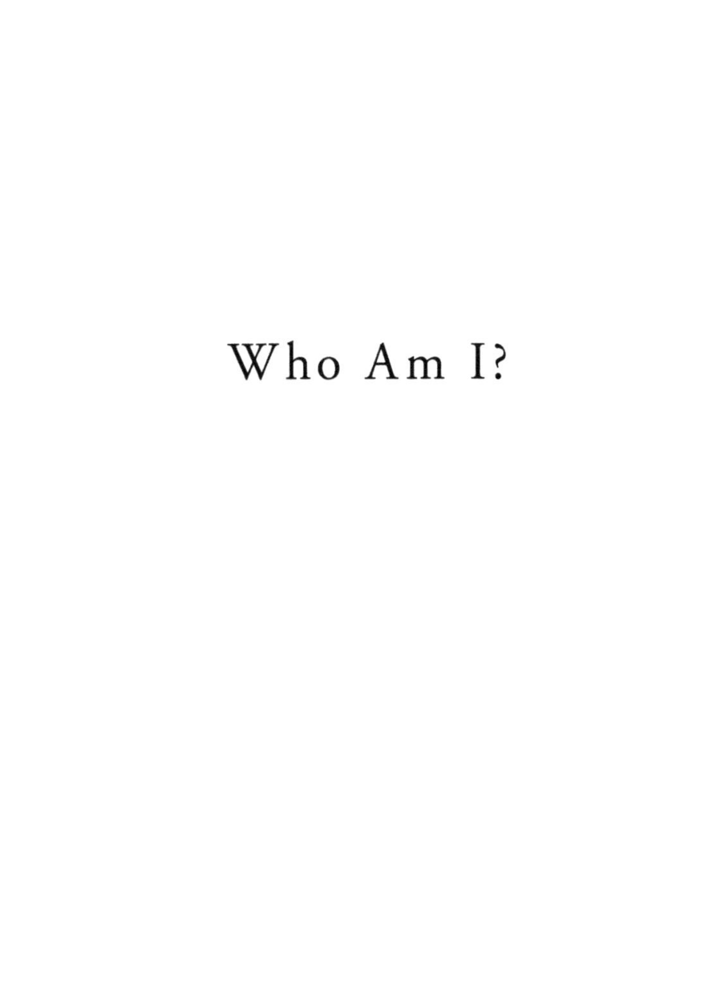

Who Am I?

"Do you know your name? Do you know who you are?" says the detached voice behind the bright light shining in my eyes. I think about the absurdity of that question; of course I know who am I.

I am the dutiful daughter of a lawyer and an accountant who attended the university of *their* choice and majored in an area of study that would make me a good living rather than going to that small liberal arts college where I could have learned how to put all the stories that were in my head on paper. The stories left me a long time ago and I haven't been able to coax them back.

I am the wife who holds her husband's hand in the movies even though it's not one I want to see. I sit in the dark sharing popcorn (not my favorite) and M&Ms with him, being with him, because it's more important to me than what's on the screen. But once in a while I'd like him to do the same for me.

I am the mother who eats lukewarm dinners after I make sure everyone else has everything they need. Often it is a dish of someone else's choosing. Tacos and chicken nuggets aren't high on my list of favorites, particularly if they've gone cold. My kids need to eat, however, and that is more important than any momentary enjoyment I would get from a nice piece of salmon.

Before I was mother, before I was wife, I was the team player in the office. I thought that maybe I could go somewhere, be somebody. But after doing the work, putting in the time and energy, someone else took the credit. It was a relief when I got pregnant and we decided that I could stay home with the baby.

Who am I? I can tell you who I am not. I am not that fussy little blonde across the street. The one who prances out of her house at seven a.m. in the cute workout gear from Lululemon, her golden hair riding high in a ponytail at the back of her head and her perfect twin daughters in tow. She drops them off at school (God forbid they should take the bus) and heads to her yoga class. Did I mention that she's a gourmet cook? Or that she's room mother for both her girls' classes? (She insisted they be placed in different rooms so they would be seen as individuals. But of course.) No, I am not her, most decidedly.

I do not wear a seven-carat diamond bridal set on my left ring finger. A simple gold band is good enough for me. At least that's what my husband seems to believe. "Think of the places we could go with that money," he says. But we never go anywhere. But the blonde does. Last year her husband sent her away to the Canyon Ranch Spa in Arizona for a week. So she could have some time to spend on herself. I get fifteen whole minutes a day in the shower. If I'm lucky.

Her name is Madison. Because of course it is. My name is Ann. Because it's simple and authoritative. So say my parents. Madisons get the guy. Anns get the guy's less-attractive friend. Madisons open the door to a fabulous arrangement of flowers "just because." Anns are lucky to get a handful of leggy pink carnations hastily purchased from the drugstore for Valentine's Day.

And Anns are the ones who look out their living room windows each morning while Madisons pack their precious girls into their Fuji White Range Rover HSEs and head off into their idyllic days. Anns are still there in their sweatpants and t-shirt when the Madisons return a few hours later, reusable bags from Whole Foods in hand, dashing in to ready a wholesome after-school snack for the twins before hopping back in the car, freshly showered, for school pick-up and ballet lessons.

I'm the one who watches as her handsome husband pulls up the driveway at six o'clock and is greeted in their large, airy kitchen by his children finishing their homework and setting the table while she gives him a kiss and hands him a scotch and soda (she'll pour herself a glass of Malbec to sip as she puts the finishing touches on dinner). I'm the one who can barely get eggs and bagels together at the end of the day. And yet I could not tell you where the time goes.

I, as an Ann, struggle through life, making do and compromising just to survive. Madisons get all the breaks. Even if a Madison is a breast cancer survivor (10 years now); these days that is more a right of passage than a real setback, isn't it? For her it will be caught early (of course) and dispatched with a lumpectomy and some chemo. In six months Madison's perfect life is restored. What would she do with real problems like the rest of us have? What would it take to crack the facade of her idyllic life?

And so I am the one who decides to test her mettle. It is me who intercepts her at the grocery store, although I avoid her as a rule because she is over-friendly. She smiles at me as if we were long-lost friends and I return the favor. We chat as we peruse overpriced organic produce and a dizzying array of supplements. I note the items in her cart: several varieties of pretentious cheeses, artisan crackers, pricey wine, and gluten-free beer mingled with the organic, low-sugar breakfast cereal and almond milk. Cocktail party. Madisons are social.

"Having a party?" I ask.

"Just a little thing," she says. "Drinks and nibbles. A few friends, a couple of neighbors. Maybe you and your husband could stop by? It's Friday at 7."

She's too polite not to invite me.

ooo

My husband, in jeans and a white button-down, brown suede driving moccasins on his feet, is dressed appropriately for the occasion. But I want to feel my best, especially when faced with the cool blonde perfection of a Madison. Camel-colored suede pants and a white silk button-down shirt. A cute pair of kitten-heeled sandals. All worn with an air of oh-I-always-dress-this-way even though sweatpants and t-shirts are my daily wardrobe. Does a Madison even own sweatpants?

This Madison answers the door dressed in a chocolate brown slouchy cashmere sweater that compliments her coloring, perfectly balanced by a pair of dark-rinse skinny jeans. Her feet are bare, her pedicure the exact shade of brown as her top. Naturally. Her hair is loose and coaxed into "beach waves." Anns are generally still upstairs in the bathroom when the guests arrive, trying in vain to find an outfit that doesn't make her feel dumpy and matronly.

We are directed to the "family room," a huge media room just off of the equally large kitchen. It is bigger than my first apartment.

I am suddenly unable to take a full breath. I excuse myself to the bathroom. My reaction is unexpected. It looks even better from the inside. Then I do what Anns do and pull myself together. As I put on fresh lipstick, there is a quiet knock on the door.

"Ann, are you okay?" Madison. "Do you need anything?" Then she whispers, "There are extra tampons under the sink."

Of course there are.

Back in control, I survey the party. On the kitchen island is a punch bowl of what looks like ginger ale with sherbet floating in it. I busy myself with a few appetizers while I watch the bowl. A woman I don't recognize—except she's a brunette version of our hostess, probably named Taylor—slides up to the counter. She smiles. "Have you tried this? It's To. Die. For. Seriously. I have to be careful not to drink too much or I'll be dancing on the tables." She waves at her gaggle of clones, trying to get their attention. When she fails, she goes to fetch them.

Despite life's hardships (or perhaps because of them), Anns are resourceful. I seize the moment. I surreptitiously grab the cups stacked nearby (plastic, Madison, really?) and hide them in the cupboard below.

As the other women search, I pull the cups back out, fill one for myself, then pour a bottle of Ipecac into the bowl.

"Look, I found them," I say to anyone who'd listen. "Madison, this punch is delicious!"

ooo

As often happens with Madisons, there is pity and understanding although her guests are up half the night vomiting. Poor Madison. She got sick too. The Mommy Brigade at school drop off Monday morning plans to get the health inspector over to Whole Foods post haste. Silly me, getting up early and carting the brood to school to witness the aftermath of what, for an Ann, would have surely been a social death, but for a Madison, is just a nauseating bump in the road.

ooo

Like any good Ann, I know when to admit defeat. Madison won. She always will. It's time to slip back into my sweatpants and close the shades on the front window. Time for life to get back to normal.

Except.

Except that she mocks me. Her continued sunny outlook and good fortune mock me. They remind me that I can't have what she's having, I can't even taste a life where everything runs smoothly and the dog doesn't throw up on the carpet three times a week. No matter how I try to avoid seeing her go about her merry way, she creeps in. I send out for groceries, arrange rides to practice for the kids and beg off social invitations. But someone has to get the mail.

Although it's raining today, the sun is beginning to peek out here and there. Madison comes out of her house in a gorgeous sky blue raincoat with coordinating Wellies. She puts the girls' ballet bags in the back of the SUV, shuts the hatch, and goes back inside. I look up and notice that there's a rainbow over her house.

ooo

I tell the voice behind the light my name, while pushing her hand away and turning my head. The light hurts. "Where am I?" ask.

"Holy Cross Hospital," the young intern replies. "You've been in a car accident."

My husband appears, his face a mixture of concern and bewilderment. The police are outside. They have questions. Apparently I was leaving the house at the same time Madison was. We were headed in the same direction. It was still raining. I accelerated suddenly, rear-ending the Range Rover and sending us both careening off the road.

"What happened?" he says. "Where were you going?"

I don't remember anything after the rainbow. My head hurts. Everything hurts. They tell me that the force of the air bag knocked me out. My chest is sore, too. And my leg is fractured in two places; I'm sporting a cast covered in bright purple. The recovery will be long. My mother will be flying in to help take care of the kids and the house—and, presumably, me. At the moment I cannot think of anything I need more or want less. Mom will have more questions than the cops. I have no answers. But I have a question of my own.

"What about Madison?" I ask.

"She's fine," comes the answer. "Walked away with just a scratch on her chin. A miracle, really…"

Missed Connection

Craigslist
New York>Manhattan>Personals>Missed Connections

Yesterday, Herald Square, F Train, Northbound Local - W4M

You: Tall, dark and handsome. Mid 40s. Wearing (well-fitting) jeans and a tailored white button-down, untucked. Butter-soft moccasins on your feet. Your curly hair slightly tousled. A man who appreciates the finer things but doesn't take it all too seriously. You were with an older woman who used a walker. I watched you with her, the way you touched her so gently, the way you smiled and whispered things to her that made her smile back. I imagined that she was your mother, and you had taken her out for a day of shopping. You were loaded down with Macy's bags and she was chatting happily, thrilled to be out and about. Her body was frail, but she had a light in her eyes that matched your own. Your tenderness and care captured my heart. I longed to cross the platform and talk to you, but I am not the sort of person who does that. I am not the sort of person who puts herself out there to attractive men because I know they will reject me. But you? Something about the way you were with her, the way you smoothed her hair and wiped the errant lipstick off the side of her mouth, told me that you were different. That you could see through the outer layers and into the soul of a woman. I checked your left ring finger for a gold band, but found none. Could it be that you are unattached?

I imagine that you are. Maybe there were a string of girlfriends, perhaps even a wife, but they didn't want to compete with your mother for your attention. You long for a woman who understands your devotion and what it means, a woman who appreciates your tenderness and care, even if it is not for her. May I introduce myself?

Me: Short, brunette and, yes, middle-aged. Growing wide in the middle, but with a beautiful, gentle heart and quick mind. I was wearing wide-legged, beige linen pants and a jean jacket. My face has never been the sort of face that men gravitate toward. A handsome woman, some might say. Time has been kind, however, as it often is to women like me. I dress to impress, to convey a confidence that I still have not managed to attain, even at this stage of my life. I am accomplished and intelligent, powerful and provocative, yet I am certain that my overtures will be rebuffed, therefore I make none. You looked at me once or twice, perhaps because I cut quite the figure out of the corner of an eye. I smiled at you, but you turned away too quickly to catch it. I willed you to turn my way again, but you focused all of your attention on her. That's what drew me to you. In a crowd of thoroughly self-contained and self-involved humanity, twenty-somethings with headphones permanently embedded in their ears, tourists attempting to decipher the subway system but afraid to ask for help, weary laborers eager to get home and begin their real lives, you stood out. You shone just as surely as God had bestowed a halo above your head. For all my accomplishments, my independence and self-sufficiency, I still long for a hero. Not the heavily muscled superhero, nor the fearless firefighter, but an everyday hero, a man for the ages. A man who's in it until the end. That image I project on you. I trust you will not disappoint.

But there's the rub, isn't it? This pedestal I've put you on is narrow and high. On it you are alone and in constant danger of falling. One muscle twitch away from crashing down to earth and laying crumpled at my feet. A disappointment. Never fear, sweet prince, I've already made you flawed. Your clothes end up on the floor more often than not, and you frequently come home late from work because you got to talking and forgot the time. Maybe you snore. I have a maid for the clothes. I'm never home before eight o'clock. I am a deep sleeper. We're a perfect match, don't you think?

We: I'm taking a chance. Sending this into the ether. Hoping that it will reach you. It's your turn to take a chance. Contact me. Give me an hour. I'll make it worth your while.

ooo

Yesterday, Herald Square, F Train, Northbound Local - M4W

I thought I'd been having a good day, out with my mother, laughing, shopping. It's so good to see her smile. She's getting older and I worry about her, so once a week we go out, anywhere she wants. To the zoo, the park or to Macy's. She loves Macy's. Has since she was a little girl. There I was with her, on the northbound platform, enjoying her company and generally feeling content when I saw you. And suddenly I realized that I've been walking around with this hole inside me for a long time. There have been women. Girls, really. Younger women who don't understand my devotion to my mother. They're just learning to fly and don't get my need to return to the nest to check in regularly. All they know is that it takes my time and attention from them. And they need a lot of attention. So when I noticed you, noticed that you had passed that particularly needy decade, it struck something inside me. It's time I found something real, something lasting. And my heart seems set on you. Why? It's in your eyes, I think. A bright, clear blue with a touch of sparkle. I see kindness there. I see heart. I see possibility. You are not my usual type, but that's exactly the point, isn't it? Did you notice me, the guy in his early 40s, with the older lady in the walker? I thought I felt you looking my way, but I didn't want to flirt in front of Mom. On her day she gets 100 percent of my attention.

You were there, across the platform, alone. You looked around, as New Yorkers do, aware of your surroundings. That's how I saw your eyes. You're tall and blonde, late thirties, lean and stylish. You had many eyes on you, but you took it in your stride, fiddling with your phone, adjusting your earbuds, seemingly oblivious to the appreciative looks. But I think I caught your eye. You may have even smiled at me once when I had turned away. You were standing next to an older woman in a jean jacket.

Get in touch. Maybe we have a future. Or maybe we can have a little fun.

Care & Feeding

Emily

There's this feeling I get when I slip into a hot bath. It pulls at my center and puts goosebumps on my skin. I've had it ever since I can remember, and it's always labeled itself when it appeared: lonesome. The instant the lower half of my body hits the hot water the feeling moves up me until the word pops into my head. Lonesome. I move through it and settle back into the tub. The feeling passes as quickly as it comes.

The weird part is, I've never been lonely before. All my life I've been the happy one, the easy one, the low-maintenance one. I've always been content with my own company. Alone is different than lonely. But put me in a tub of just-this-side-of-scalding water, and the intense ache of loneliness fills me up—if only for a few seconds. Could it be a primal sense memory, a longing to be back in the womb?

It was surprising to me the first time I felt this particular tug on my heart outside of the bathtub. I recognized it right away. I was propped up in our king-sized bed, reading the latest Linda Fairstein bestseller. Jeff was parked in front of the television, binge-watching something I had no interest in. I had just finished chapter three when it hit me, right in the heart. Lonesome. I suddenly felt lonesome. But this time it didn't pass so quickly. It kind of took my breath away. I reached over and pulled my French bulldog, Chloe, to my lap and buried my face in her neck, breathing her scent. Funny how other people's dogs just smell like dog, but our own have a special essence that's as distinctive as a lover's. But that night even a big whiff of Chloe and the sound of her snuffling couldn't make me feel better. I had to face it. Three years into the marriage of my dreams, the bottom had dropped out. I wasn't alone, but my heart didn't know that.

Jeff

The best thing about my marriage? The food. I'm not kidding; it's amazing. A couple of Christmases ago Em's dad gave her a subscription to a gourmet food service. Her parents are wealthy—like private plane wealthy. They gave us a house as a wedding present. Anyway, the food. Seven days worth of the most insane food you'd could ever imagine, delivered right to our door every Monday morning. Have you ever had pastries made with real butter? My mom was strictly margarine growing up so that was a shocker—in a good way.

The worst thing about my marriage? I'm not sure you can even call it a marriage anymore. It was great in the beginning, really great. But then it wasn't. I started working on my master's degree, taking classes and studying nights and weekends. Em's girls' nights went from one or two a month to a weekly thing. Date nights slowly petered out. We exist on different planes, circulate in different orbits.

I looked up from my thesis one night and realized the house was really quiet. And very dark except for a pool of light from my desk lamp and the cool glow of my laptop. It was four in the morning. I'd been working since seven the night before. I didn't remember Emily coming home from work or taking Chloe on her evening walk (something we used to do together). Did she even come home that night? I found her in our bedroom, sound asleep; she probably had been since eleven o'clock. I hadn't even known she was there. But I did notice earlier that the last apple turnover was gone.

Emily

He mentioned the food? Huh. I've always wondered if Jeff has a problem with my parents' money. He forgets that it's my parents' money, not mine. They paid for my college education, but it stopped there. I've been on my own since graduation. I've eaten ramen noodles every night for weeks to make rent after impulsively treating a friend to a dinner I couldn't afford. No one bailed me out; I wouldn't even have thought to ask. Sure, they've given me some extravagant gifts, like our house and the cleaning service, both for our wedding—which Jeff and I paid for— but on a day-to-day basis, we live on what we earn. Mom and Dad gave us the house so we'd have a solid financial base (they believe in the value of real estate). It's a modest house, not a McMansion. A fixer-upper really. But it is in a great neighborhood, which makes it a solid investment. The maid service was to keep us from fighting about chores since we both work long hours.

So, the food. About a year after we got married, my parents gave us this weekly gourmet food service thing. It was something my father was thinking about investing in, and we were going to be the guinea pigs. But that wasn't the only reason they gave it to us. I had recently gotten pregnant and they wanted to make sure we didn't have to worry about feeding ourselves when we had a newborn to take care of. My mother always told me that the best gifts she got after I was born were the plates of food the neighbors brought over. She didn't have to even think about dinner for weeks. It is a brilliant gift, really. And the food was wonderful; Jeff is right about that.

Yes, we stopped cooking together after that. But we didn't stop connecting. That didn't happen because we didn't pull a pot or pan out of the cupboard for weeks on end or have to chop onions and garlic anymore. And it didn't happen slowly either. It wasn't subtle or gradual. It was abrupt. Sudden. And incredibly painful.

Jeff

Okay, yes, I was a little put off by the house, but I got over it. There's no way we could have afforded it, even now. It was paid for in full, and we were able to borrow against the value to do the renovations. Now it's worth almost twice what it sold for. It was a really great wedding gift.

And the food service, that just made sense. Em was tired all the time when she was pregnant, so it made things easier. She was sick a lot, too. Not at all how I'd imagined it. In my mind Em would be glowing and happy, growing a little baby bump that I could talk to and read to. I had no idea it could be so rough on her. She just wasn't herself. She tried so hard to be upbeat, but most of the time she was too tired to move after working all day. I had to drag her out of bed in the morning, which was not like her. It was different, but it was okay. We were having a baby.

I remember everything about that night. It was a Thursday. We were getting ready for bed. I heard her crying in the bathroom. She was bleeding. I think she was about 11 or 12 weeks along at that point. She was scared. So was I. I told her we'd call the doctor in the morning if it didn't stop. She took some Tylenol for the cramping and we went to bed. The next thing I knew she was waking me up and telling me we needed to get to the hospital right away. There was blood on the sheets. Em looked as white as a ghost; I could tell she was in a lot of pain. And terrified.

We sat in the hallway of the ER for a while because there were no rooms available. Em was still bleeding, but it didn't seem to be enough to concern anyone too much. She laid there on a gurney. They took her blood and monitored her each time she went to the bathroom. It wasn't until about 7 a.m. that we found out for sure that she had a miscarriage.

Emily

We got home from the hospital that afternoon and headed right to bed. Jeff seemed to sleep just fine, but I tossed and turned for hours. In my head I rewound the whole night over and over. I could not get out of the ER. I could not forget that I'd lost our baby. Later I realized it was the after-effects of the anesthesia from the D&C that had me caught in that horror loop. After a while I didn't want to sleep anymore. I couldn't keep going back there.

Jeff took good care of me. He made sure I was fed, and that I had my prescription. He made me a bed on our couch and we watched old movies together for the rest of the evening. We huddled together under a blanket, but we didn't speak much.

Jeff

It was cloudy that day, I remember, but it never rained. It was a quiet afternoon that turned into a quiet evening. By the next morning it was even quieter. We had both slid down into separate pits of despair. I felt like there was a weight on my chest all the time. It didn't go away in the weeks that followed. There was a part of me that seemed to be missing, but I didn't know what it was. I imagined that Emily felt the same way; I didn't ask her.

Emily

I pulled away after that, I know I did. It had been a bad pregnancy right from the start—the depression settled in right along with the morning sickness—but then at least I had the thought of a baby at the end. And when that was gone, all that was left was the sad. I have never felt so empty as I did right after my miscarriage. It was as if my soul had left my body along with the baby. Nobody was coming in, not even my mom, but especially not Jeff. When we were together the pain just doubled. That's not how it's supposed to be, is it?

Jeff

Chloe was an impulse. Emily was so distant, so depressed, and I was just numb. And then we saw her. The pet store near our supermarket was having an adoption event. We walked over to look at the dogs and there she was, this tiny thing with bat ears and a big smile on her face when she saw Emily. It was love at first sight for both of them. We had to take her home.

Emily

I poured all of my love, all of my want, into that little dog. We both spoiled her. She wanted for nothing. Still doesn't. She helped lift us out of our depression. I began to feel better, to get back, bit by bit, into life. So did Jeff. The trouble was we didn't do it together. We were living parallel lives, and we didn't seem to notice or care. I guess I thought it was part of the healing process and that when it was done we'd go back to normal. Except that normal was completely and utterly different. The child didn't even have a chance to be born, wasn't much more than a blob on an ultrasound screen and yet it had changed me, altered my DNA. I was not the same person I'd been just weeks before. Neither was Jeff.

Jeff

And that's how we've been ever since. Emily's not the same person I fell in love with; I guess I'm not the same person she fell in love with. There is a line in our lives: Before and after. Before, we were in love. After, we are wounded and wary, with our hearts walled off so we don't get hurt anymore.

But I want a family. I want kids, not just a dog. I want a wife, not just a roommate. But there is that line. And I'm afraid to move past it.

Emily

It took a long time before I could see a pregnant woman and not get angry. Or a new mom and not want to cry. But it took me even longer to want to try again. But I need my marriage back first. I know it's never going to be the same as it was, but after what we've been through together maybe we can be stronger. But someone is going to have to take that first step.

Jeff

I guess it's time to move forward, isn't it?

Emily

Maybe if we both took that step together…

Stranger on a Bus

I killed my baby. I had to. I didn't want anything to tie me to him forever. So before I even told him I was pregnant, I took care of it. All it took was a few cups of "miscarriage tea" that a friend got me from an herbalist. In a few days the cramping started. One bad period later, it was done.

Maybe you think I'm a monster, or a stupid, irresponsible kid. I get it. I would too. But there are things you don't know. About me. About him.

Why would I tell a stranger these things? Because I have to tell someone. It weighs on me and I have to lessen the load. You don't know me, don't care that much about my life or anything; it's not a burden to you. So I'll tell you.

He beats me. A lot. Right up until last night. He's cracked my ribs, fractured my collarbone and given me a concussion. He loves me, he says, but he has no idea what love is. I don't know what it is that he feels about me, but I know that he thinks I belong to him, the same way his car or his favorite pair of Levi's do. Like I'm one of those sex dolls that look almost like real women. Real Girls, I think that's what they're called. He gets angry with me for being an actual live woman, with thoughts and feelings and dreams.

Were the signs there when we started dating? I suppose. A bunch of little things, nothing by themselves, but looking back they say it all. I was naive. And in love. They don't teach you what to look for when they're telling you about boys. And you wouldn't believe them anyway because you know it will never happen to you. You like a guy and realize that he's not perfect, that he has these quirks that you have to put up with—but everybody does. Then you wake up one morning with a black eye and wonder how you ended up there.

Of course I thought it was my fault; he certainly wasn't taking the blame. I was doing it wrong. All of it. If I could only learn, things would be better. I tried. God, did I try. I reinvented myself more than once. Changed my hair and my clothes, learned his favorite recipes from his mom. But it was never right. It finally dawned on me that it would never be right.

How do you bring a baby into that? I'm not even sure that he would want a child. He probably would have made me get an abortion anyway; a baby would take my attention away from him.

I was afraid one day he'd beat me so badly that I'd miscarry. Ironic, huh? But I didn't want to fall in love with that tiny creature, then have him take it away. And what kind of father would he be? What would I be subjecting my little one to?

Why did I stay with him? I don't love him. Maybe once, for five minutes. But that was a long time ago. I stayed because if I tried to go, he would kill me. I was sure of that. I've thought about leaving for a long time, but I could never figure out how to keep him from hunting me down and beating me to death right where he found me.

How did I get away? I killed myself. Staged my own death. All that blood from the abortion, a few well-placed clues. I left everything and everyone behind. The best part is that they'll think he did it. I left a few breadcrumbs leading his way. Everyone knows what he his, what he does to me. But they were all too scared to help.

So I'm not me anymore. I'm someone else. My hair is different, my clothes are different. I don't even know who she is yet; it's only been a few hours. She lives far away, someplace I never heard of before. And she is strong. Independent. Nobody's punching bag. And maybe one day she'll have a baby.

Minus One Day

"I'm going to kill myself," says Tracey. It's a gray November day a week before Thanksgiving. The only light in the room is from a lamp she brought from home because the hospital's fluorescent lighting is cold and depressing. She sits in an uncomfortable metal chair pulled up to slightly less uncomfortable hospital bed where her best friend, Robyn, is lying.

"Why?" says Robyn, taking Tracey's hand. She has the blankets pulled up to her chin and wears a scarf wrapped around her head even though there's no one here to horrify with her "bald chemo head."

"I don't want to be here without you." Tracey's voice breaks and she looks down at her lap while raising Robyn's hand to her lips. She doesn't want to cry in front of Robyn, doesn't want to feel sorry for herself. She's not the one whose insides are being eaten away by cancer. She's perfectly healthy, if not still young. Seventy is the new 50, right? Or whatever age you are is the new age that you'd really rather be.

"You'll get used to it. Now stop being a drama queen."

Tracey looks up. "No, I mean it, Rob. If you're not here, what's the point?"

Robyn doesn't have a good answer. She can't imagine her life without her best friend either. But the world is a better place with

Tracey in it, that much she knows. The thought of this woman gone makes her angry, angrier than she already is at dying before she's finished here. She hits the button on the bed so she can sit up and look Tracey in the eye. "If you kill yourself I will never forgive you."

"You won't be here."

"But I'll know. And I'll be pissed. Who's going to tell me what's going on with the Kardashians?"

"You don't think they have TMZ in Heaven?"

Robyn looks at Tracey pointedly. "How could it be Heaven with TMZ there?"

ooo

1967. Weight Watchers' nine a.m. Wednesday meeting at the Lynbrook Recreation Center. Tracey was three months post-baby, a beautiful little girl she named Susan. She was still carrying around an extra 20 pounds and no matter how many times her mother told her that "it took nine months to put it on; it will take nine months to take it off," she couldn't stand to look in the mirror. "Hormones," her mother said. Whatever, she thought, they need to go if I ever want to have sex again. She simply wouldn't let Tony see her naked until she was back down to her fighting weight. He wasn't happy. Neither was she. The Weight Watchers flyer on the board in the A&P seemed like a sign to her. She got her mom to sit with Susan so she could go. "What's the hurry?" Mom asked. It had probably been so long since her mother had sex she'd forgotten all about it. But Tracey hadn't and she missed it. A lot. Almost enough to just go ahead and do it before she lost the weight. Maybe if the lights were off and she kept her nightgown on? Not sexy, Trace, she thought. Not. Sexy.

She'd arrived ten minutes early. The door was open, but there was nobody around. She sat down in the first row of metal folding chairs facing a rolling chalkboard at one end of the room. Tracey laughed at herself; still the dutiful pupil, sitting front and center, composition book and pencil in hand. She'd always been a perfect

104

child, a perfect student, a perfect wife. Suddenly she felt very tired. She moved to a row in middle.

Members began to trickle in. Some were thin, some were chubby and some were downright fat. Tracey hoped the fat ones were new to the program. She needed this to work.

"Scoot over," she heard from above her head. The whiskey voice belonged to a beautiful brunette with a sleek Vidal Sassoon bob. She was wearing hot pink petal pushers and a floral sleeveless top, and she was smiling down at Tracey. The brunette was not model thin, but she wasn't one of the bigger girls either. Tracey moved over one seat.

"Hiya, I'm Robyn," she said once she was settled in the chair.

Tracey nodded. "Tracey," she said.

"T-R-A-C-Y?" Robyn asked as she rifled through her handbag.

"No, E-Y."

"A-ha! I knew I had some gum in here somewhere," Robyn said, popping a stick of Juicy Fruit in her mouth. "I'm starving. You want?" She thrust the pack toward Tracey.

"No, thank you."

"Suit yourself. But you'll wish you had this when they start talking about food. Just nudge me and I'll slip you a piece." She put the gum back in her purse. "So how come E-Y?"

"Pardon?"

"You have beautiful manners." Robyn waved the air, dismissing the comment. "Why is your name spelled with an E-Y?"

Tracey thought for a moment. "I don't know."

Robyn laughed. "My parents would have preferred having you for a daughter," she said. "My name is spelled R-O-B-Y-N; I started asking why the first day of Kindergarten when Mrs. James insisted that it was wrong. It took my mother three years to admit she was so doped up after I was born that she misspelled it."

"Really?"

"Hand to God. At first she told me that my father didn't want me named after a bird, which is actually true. He also didn't want anyone calling me 'Rob' for short. Heh, as soon as I heard that I wouldn't answer to anything else.

"Anyway, I knew she was lying, so I kept pestering her. Finally I got her when she'd had a couple of grasshoppers and she confessed. She was so embarrassed. I thought it was hysterical."

Tracey smiled. "It is pretty funny." She looked down at her notebook. Say something else, she thought. "So how long have you been coming here?"

"Years. I keep gaining and losing the same twenty pounds." Robyn tossed her hair and turned to Tracey, who looked horrified. She put a hand on Tracey's wrist. "I keep getting knocked up," she laughed.

ooo

"It's freezing in here," Robyn says, pulling the blanket tighter around her.

"It's 75 degrees." Tracey gets up. "Shove over," she says as she climbs into the bed. She lies down next to Robyn and puts her arms around her friend. "Better?"

"Yeah."

"Who's going to be around to do this for me if I get sick? I'll die with blue lips and cold feet." Tracey settles her head on Robyn's shoulder and inhales her scent, a heady combination of baby powder and Chanel No 5 that Tracey has been unable to duplicate in 47 years. The smell would never stick to her; no perfume ever did. Once, as a joke, she dabbed Pine Sol behind her ears. Five women insisted on knowing what she was wearing. "It's perfect," said one.

"Susan will. That's why we have kids: To tend to us in our old age." She pats Tracey's hand. "Or ship us off to a home."

ooo

"March sixth, 1973, a day that will live in infamy…" Robyn was resting her head on the window of Tracey's VW Beetle as they crawled down the street, looking for the address on the scrap of paper Tracey held in her hand.

"Shush, I'm trying to concentrate," Tracey said. They were in Queens, out of their Long Island comfort zone. "I've never been here before."

"And I have?" Robyn snapped. She turned to her friend. "You think I do this every day? Is that what you think of me?"

Tracey stopped the car. "Of course not! I didn't mean anything. I'm just a little nervous. This is not the best neighborhood…"

Robyn looked around at the dingy buildings that lined the street. "This is exactly the type of neighborhood my mother was always afraid I'd be found dead in when I was a teenager. Today her dream might come true, just a few years late."

"Stop it, Rob. You'll be fine. He was highly recommended."

"Assuming we even make it in the door. I think that bum over there is dead." Robyn pointed to what appeared to be a heap of dirty clothes with a filthy gray beard. "We've passed him five times and he hasn't moved an inch."

Tracey looked around again. "Do you think there's a pay phone nearby? Maybe we could call…"

"Who are we going to call? Information?" She mimed a telephone with her pinky and thumb and brought it to her ear. "Yes, hello? I was wondering if you could give me the address of the illegal abortionist in Ozone Park?"

"Shhhh! Don't say that out loud!"

"Who's going to hear me, the dead guy?" Robyn pointed out the window with her thumb. "You need to calm down, Trace. You're not the one getting the abortion. Who am I going to lean on if you fall apart?"

"Are you sure you want to do this? Maybe you should talk to Mike. He could probably find a doctor who'll say you need a procedure…"

"No way. Mike is more Catholic than the Pope. If it were up to him, I'd have three more. He always wanted six kids. Ugh. And here I was worried that he'd find my birth control pills. Ha! I didn't even get to take the first one. You're supposed to wait for your period to start them. Woman plans, man comes home from a bachelor party, God laughs."

"You're sure, then?"

Robyn looked out the window again. "I can't have another one. I can't." Her voice broke. After a moment she turned back to Tracey. "I can't go to Weight Watchers again. Give me the address."

Tracey handed over the paper.

"It's right there, across the street," said Robyn, pointing out the front window. "With the blue door."

"Oh, yeah," Tracey said, shoulders sagging. She took a deep breath and turned to Robyn with a smile. "You ready?"

"Yeah, sure. Thanks, Trace. You're saving my life. Or killing me. We'll know in a couple of hours."

"Jesus, Robyn," Tracey said as she opened the door.

"Don't take the Lord's name in vain," Robyn called after her. "It's a sin."

Tracey poked her head back in the car. "Seriously?"

Robyn shrugged.

ooo

"Know what I am going to miss the most when I'm gone?" Robyn says as she turns to face her friend.

"What's that?" Tracey asks. Her eyes are closed and she's in that place between sleep and waking. Hospitals exhaust her.

"A really good foot rub. Mike used to give the best foot rubs. His hands were strong and he didn't get tired too fast. God, it was better than sex. That's why I always got a pedicure every week after he died." Mike had died ten years ago and she still missed him every day. *If not for Tracey*, she thought, *I'd have died too.*

Tracey opens her eyes and sits up. "Hang on a sec," she says as she walks out of the room. She returns a few minutes later carrying a bottle of lotion. "I borrowed this from the nurse's station. Don't let me forget to bring it back or they might 'forget' your pain meds." She moves her chair to the end of the bed, uncovers Robyn's feet, loads up her hands with lotion and starts to massage the left foot.

Robyn closes her eyes and sighs. "You are a good woman."

"I learned from the best."

ooo

Robyn threw open the curtains in Tracey's bedroom. "Wake up; it's 1985," she said, clapping her hands. "You've been asleep for six years!"

"Wake me again at the turn of the century," Tracey said, rolling over and pulling the covers over her head.

"Susan will be in her thirties by then. And probably married to Bobby Miller. With a couple of kids. Don't you want to see your grandchildren be born?"

Tracey rolled over. "Bobby Miller is awful. Why in the world would Susan marry him?"

Robyn mimed a pregnant belly with her hands. "Your mother refused to have 'the talk' with her, so she let Bobby get past third base. PS, she walked down the aisle trying not to throw up from morning sickness. And it's all your fault."

"Susan's smarter than that. And if she's not, what the hell could I have done about it?"

"Been there for her." Robyn knelt down beside the bed. "I know it's hard, hon, but you've got to get on with it and make a life for you and Susan. You guys were the loves of Tony's life; he wouldn't want you to give up just because he's gone. You don't even have to do it all at once. Even if you just get out of bed today and take a shower, that will be enough.

"I brought over a couple of trays of lasagna, some spaghetti and meatballs, and that eggplant dish that you like. You won't have to cook for weeks."

"Thanks, but I'm not hungry."

"It's for Susan. I brought this for you." She tossed a bottle of Smirnoff and a carton of Marlboros on the bed.

Tracey thought for a moment. "There's some OJ in the fridge. I'll meet you there in a few minutes."

ooo

The light outside the window is fading, and the hospital room has grown too dark for the little table lamp. As she covers Robyn's feet and stretches her tired hands, Tracey asks her if she's ready for the overhead lights.

Robyn puts her arm over her eyes. "No, but do it anyway." As the bulbs flicker on, she says, "I wonder if we could put a scarf over that fixture to filter the light."

"You're the handy one, not me. And before you ask, there is no way in hell I'm letting you climb on the furniture to do it." Tracey moves the chair back to the side of the bed and sits down.

"Mikey Jr. is coming tomorrow," Robyn says, looking up at the light. "I'll get him to do it. Just remember to bring me that light blue scarf in the morning."

"Blue? You want the room to be blue?"

"Light blue. It's a happy color."

"I'll bring the peach one. It's sheer and will warm up the room. Trust me."

Robyn sighs. "I want to go home."

"I know," Tracey says, taking her hand. "Have you talked to Lisa again?"

"Every day. But she's insisting I stay here." She looks out the window. "Trace, I don't want to die in this place."

Tracey gets up to stretch her back. She walks to the window and looks out into the night. "Remind me why you signed over Power of Attorney to her."

"I really thought I'd be out of it by now," Robyn says. "She's the oldest, and the most responsible. It made sense. But she's just freaking out, which really surprised me. I think she thinks if I'm here they can keep me alive."

"She knows about the Do Not Resuscitate, right?"

"Yeah. But I know she thinks she can overrule it." Robyn sits up and props her elbows on her knees and her head in her hands. She's quiet for a few moments, then she pops her head up. "And this is why you can't kill yourself," she says, pointing at Tracey. "You have to talk to Lisa; you have to get me home so I can go peacefully, in a comfortable bed. So I can say goodbye to Snickers for God's sake."

"That poor cat. He sleeps in your bed every night. He misses you like crazy." Tracey crosses to the bed and sits down. "I'll talk to her, Rob. I'll make her understand. I'll get you home."

ooo

"The least Mike could have done was wait until after Valentine's Day to die," said Robyn. She and Tracey were standing in the walk-in closet of the bedroom she'd shared with her husband for almost four decades. "He knew it was my favorite holiday. Now? Not so much." She dumped the last of the ties into a box and walked into the bedroom. "I'm selling the house."

Tracey dragged the box to the door. "Make sure Mikey Jr. takes this to the car for you. The last thing you need is to throw your back out." She sat down on the bed. "Why are you selling?"

"It's too big. The kids are gone. We were talking about selling and buying a little place on the North Shore. Plus, I can't afford it. The taxes will wipe me out."

"No life insurance?" Tracey knew that after he retired, Mike became a frequent visitor to the race track. He'd always been a gambler, but it had become a problem in the last few years.

Robyn shook her head and sat down next to her friend. "We cashed that in a while back."

"You know, I've always wanted to live on the North Shore. Port Jefferson maybe. Huntington. I bet if we pooled our resources…"

"You'd sell your place? Really?"

"In a New York minute. It was never my taste anyway. Tony's parents bought it for us. Furnished it too. Sell it all, I say. Between the two of us we can probably buy something decent. And maybe we can afford to have a girl come and clean every week."

"Wouldn't that be something?" Robyn said, lying back on the bed. "I'm so sick of cleaning. I've been doing it more than half my life. Can you believe the line of crap we were fed? 'Get married, start a family, keep a home … '. They never told you that you'd probably outlive your husband, rendering you completely useless just when you're too old to go out and a real job."

"Or that your boobs would slide down to your navel."

"What about your mother?" Robyn asked. "Didn't you ever notice hers?"

"I can't prove it, but I think my mother wore a bra in the shower. A girdle too."

ooo

"Hit me," Robyn says, eyeing the cards sitting in front of her on the hospital tray table. They're playing Blackjack, not for money, but for calcium chews. Tracey is addicted to them and eats them like candy. "My bones are probably like concrete by now," she says.

Robyn pops a Godiva chocolate cigar in her mouth and pretends to smoke it. "God, I miss cigarettes almost as much as I miss Mike," she says.

Tracey nods and bites the tip off of her cigar. "I was planning on starting up again when I was 80," she says.

They play a couple of more hands in silence. It's a comfortable silence, one that doesn't need to be broken with talk about the weather or the television show of the moment. It's the silence of people who know each other's secrets and dreams, the kind that is a conversation all on its own.

"Aren't you afraid?" says Robyn.

Tracey looks up from her cards. "Of what?"

"Dying. Doesn't it scare you?"

"Does it really matter? It's coming regardless of how I feel about it."

"I can't imagine ending my own life. I'd do anything to get a few more good years."

Tracey covers Robyn's hand with her own. "I'm more scared of going on without my best friend. Life after you're gone is just ... nothing. I can't even visualize it. There's no light, no laughter, nothing."

"You have to bring your own light. There's so much out there, but you have to look for it; it won't come to you."

"Why does it matter to you whether or not I'm here after you're gone?" Tracey's throat tightens. She hates thinking about Robyn's death. She doesn't want to be there to see the life drain from the woman who's been her anchor for almost 50 years.

"I don't know. I guess I hate the thought of you not being here. There aren't too many people like you around; you make here better." There are tears in her eyes. "Plus, if we go around the same time they'll have our memorials together, and dammit, if I can't be the center of attention at my own funeral, what's the point?"

ooo

Another hospital room, about a year before. After Robyn's surgery. The cancer had spread. The odds were not good. Tracey held Robyn hands in her own. She had so much to say, but she couldn't find the words. *This cannot be where it ends*, she thought. *There are miles left to go.* They'd been planning to eat their way through Italy in the fall. "The best part about being 70 is that no one cares if you have a waistline or not," said Robyn. There was that sign language class at the Recreation Center to take. Robyn wasn't particularly interested until Tracey pointed out that they could talk about people at parties from across the room.

"The good news is, I've probably lost a few pounds. After the chemo, I'll probably be able to fit into that cute little Pucci dress Mike bought me for our honeymoon," said Robyn.

"It's a mini dress," said Tracey.

"What? My legs are still good," Robyn said, pulling one out from under the sheet and holding it up for Tracey to see.

"The varicose veins will clash with the pattern."

Robyn jabbed her finger at Tracey. "I've been waiting for 40 years to get back into that damn dress, and I'm wearing it."

They were quiet for a few minutes, lost in their own thoughts. A nurse came in and checked Robyn's vitals and explained how to use the pain pump. She asked if there was anything else they needed.

"A miracle," said Tracey without thinking. She turned back to her friend, who, for the first time since her diagnosis, looked appropriately freaked out.

"This is a punishment isn't it?" Robyn said quietly. "For the abortion."

"Oh, honey, no. Of course not." Tracey stroked Robyn's brow.

"Then why me?" Tears rolled down her face.

Tracey wiped them away. "You probably took the Lord's name in vain one too many times," she said.

ooo

A nurse pops her head into the room to remind Tracey that visiting hours are almost over. "Five minutes," she says, tapping the door jamb for emphasis.

"So when is it going to be?" Robyn asks, looking down at her hands.

"What?"

"The suicide. When are you going to do it?" Her voice is weak, almost reedy, and most definitely not Robyn-like.

Tracey shrugs. "I don't know yet. It depends on you." She leans in and puts her elbows on the bed. "I promise I won't leave until you won't know I'm gone. If I time it right, one day before you do."

Robyn smiles. "Winnie-the-Pooh." She frowns. "But it was supposed to be one hundred years." Tears well up in her eyes.

"I'll take what I can get," Tracey says, pulling her friend's head toward hers so their foreheads touch. "But I don't want to live a day without you."

Robyn pulls away. "But you have to. For me."

Tracey looks at her, confused.

"Look, I know how you feel, I do. If the situation was reversed I'd probably want to do the same. But don't, Trace. Please. Don't leave my kids alone. I need them to know me. You know all my stories. Be here to tell them."

And there it was, the only thing that could have given Tracey pause. Robyn's kids. And Susan. She would be the sole keeper of their childhoods, their history. As long as she could tell the stories, the kids wouldn't lose their mother completely. But still, the pain of not seeing Robyn's face again, of not hearing that voice or seeing her standing there with her hands on her hips and her sarcasm on high, seems too much to bear.

"I'll think about it," she says.

"Time to go." The nurse pokes her head in the doorway.

Tracey gets up and sits on the bed to hug Robyn. "See you tomorrow, kid."

"I'm counting on it," says Robyn. "I think I'm going to make a run for it tomorrow and I need someone to create a distraction. And make sure my ass isn't hanging out of the back of this gown."

"You got it."

Acknowledgements

This book was a labor of love, not only for me, but for the amazing people who stepped up to help me make it a reality. I couldn't have done any of this without the love and encouragement of my husband, Mitch. He reads it all before anyone else and keeps me sane.

A huge thank you to Stef Ploof for being the ultimate crash test dummy; she read every story and offered some of the best suggestions I've ever gotten.

A great debt of gratitute also goes to my fearless beta readers: Bud Buckley, Shari Caputo, Rachel Cohen, Chris Hutton, and Holly Hutton. Your thoughts, input, and encouragement kept me going through this process.

Robin Mills, Britt Reints, Suzy Soro, and Shephard Summers, your advice and wisdom was enourmously helpful in shaping what this little book became.

To my mother, Kathy Cooper, thanks for... well, everything.

And to you, reader, thank you for taking a chance and spending some of your time with my words.

About The Author

Megan Gordon has been writing and editing other people's words for over two decades. Now she's following her own muse and sharing her unique perspective. In her first anthology, she is turning her practiced eye to the moments that make a life and the choices, mistakes and triumphs that shape them.

Connect with Megan:
megangordonwriting.com
facebook.com/authormegangordon
twitter.com/msmegan